# *The* Hero Within

## Volume One

# Awareness

## Yeral E. Ogando

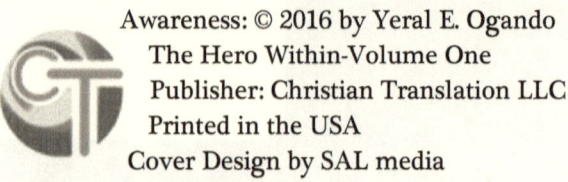

Awareness: © 2016 by Yeral E. Ogando
The Hero Within-Volume One
Publisher: Christian Translation LLC
Printed in the USA
Cover Design by SAL media

Scripture quotations are from the King James Version of the Bible.

ISBN 13: 978-0996687317
ISBN 10: 0996687319

Library of Congress Cataloging-in-Publication Data
Ogando, Yeral E.
*Title*: /Awareness
ISBN 0-9966873-1-9  (paperback)

1. Series Fiction  2. Spiritual Warfare  3. Christian .4. Inspirational

I. Title. Library of Congress Control Number: 2016904387

## DEDICATION:

This book is dedicated to the Unique and forever-lasting person who has always been there for me, no matter how stubborn I am:

GOD

I also want to dedicate this work to YOU (the reader), because you have taken the moment to read this incredible story and without you I would not have been here.

You all have a special place in my heart.

Always.

# ACKNOWLEDGMENTS:

Thanks to God for allowing my dream to come true, and for giving me strength when I felt like giving up.

Had it not been for the support that I have received along the way from these incredible and amazing people, I would not be where I am today.

Thanks to my editor, Sharon A. Lavy and SAL media "Cover Design" for doing such a great job helping me polish this book.

Barry Napier for his excellent work: writing, brainstorming, encouraging, and keeping me on track during the creation of this first book in the series.

Thanks to Marilyn K. Smith for her wonderful imagination and continuing help while we completed the vision of Awareness.

And I can't forget to mention Matthew & Traci Elliott for their continuous support of The Hero Within series.

This has been a very long ride for my family, but the reward is worthy. Thanks to my father, Hector and my daughters, Yeiris & Tiffany for staying by my side through this journey. You know I love you.

# CHAPTER 1

Anthony Markson sat on the barstool nursing his fifth beer of the evening, when his iPhone binged an alert.

*Coming to church with me in the morning?*

Shish. Not likely. He slipped the cell into his right front trouser pocket.

The stinky-sweet smells of the bar were starting to get to him, and he figured he should stop after this one. Anyway, he was pretty sure the bartender was watering down his drinks.

Besides, Becky would worry about him if he wasn't home soon. The sun had set 20 minutes ago, and it wasn't long till darkness would fall.

*The Rat's Nest Bar* was Anthony's favorite place to let down. The hole in the wall was one place he could be incognito, and where people only knew him as Tony.

Since this was his only real relaxation for the week, was it too much to ask for a few hours on Saturday night?

The Hispanic bartender eyed Anthony's nearly empty glass. "Another one?" he asked.

Anthony was tempted, but shook his head. "Better

not. The old lady will raise a ruckus if I don't leave soon." It simply wasn't worth putting up with the guilt and ridicule he might find at home.

The tender nodded. "I hear that. You better keep that one happy."

Anthony eyed the man. Did he know Becky? "Can you bring my tab?"

"Sure thing." The man walked to the register leaving Anthony to stare into the dregs of his beer. Did Becky ever regret marrying an Angelo?

He raised the glass to his lips and finished it off, desperately fighting the craving to have a sixth, and a seventh, and an eighth.

Maybe if he switched to lite beer? Nah.

Anthony ambled to the checkout and paid his tab before the cravings could win the fight. He didn't look forward to arguing with his wife or seeing the disappointed gleam in his son's brown eyes. He knew how much Ben wanted to go to the baseball game tomorrow.

He weaved his way out of the bar and into the parking lot to find his car.

No sooner had he slid the keys into the ignition, when his phone buzzed again. Anthony rolled his eyes, sure it was his sister, Janet. She just wouldn't give up trying to pester him into coming to church with her. Not just him, either, but Becky and Ben, too.

She really ought to get a life. But as an

unmarried school teacher she'd taken over his family as her pet project.

He almost didn't bother checking the message. But when he did, his stomach lurched.

Deep-seeded guilt spiraled through him as he saw the simple message from Becky: *When will you be home?*

For a moment, the buttons on his phone swam in the air. And as Anthony typed a message back to his wife, he realized he was a bit more inebriated than he'd realized.

He had to correct the text twice, but he finally got it typed. *In the car now. Headed home.*

With a feeling of accomplishment, he pushed send.

Almost immediately, she responded back. *Be careful.*

Anthony didn't know if it was possible, but he could swear there was some condescension in her message.

Be careful, in this case, meant she knew he'd probably had too much to drink and had no business behind the wheel.

He smirked. Little did she know, he'd driven home in much worse shape several times before.

Still, once Anthony pulled out of the bar's parking lot and onto the familiar streets that would carry him home, he made sure to drive the speed limit. He didn't want anything happening to the paint job on his Porsche.

Ten blocks later, he made it home without incident or accident. Now it was time to face the music.

He pulled his car into the two-car garage and checked his watch. The trip from *The Rat's Nest* to his house took twenty minutes, and at the moment it was not much after 9:00 o'clock.

Suddenly deflated, Anthony felt he was wasting a perfectly good Saturday night. Actually, he felt a rant coming on.

Thirteen years ago, just out of Law school, before he and Becky had gotten married, they would have been out late, hanging with friends, not at all worried about waking up early enough to make it to a baseball game that neither of them wanted to attend. Why did all that have to change?

But then again, he reasoned with himself, Becky hadn't been with him tonight. He hadn't been out partying with her. She deserved some quality time with him, and he hated the way his rants turned into pity parties.

And Ben. Of course, Anthony loved his son to no end. The boy was looking forward to the game. He was so infatuated with baseball.

But there were times when he looked at the six-year-old, and he wondered if he'd left the better years of his life far behind him. No more partying, no more irresponsible drinking. No. Now it was a wife, a kid, and a nice house in the suburbs. What a drag.

Janet wouldn't be impressed with his pity party. She'd told him time and time again he was blessed—that he had a blest life. He supposed he understood how someone as uninformed as his sister could see it that way.

Because Janet lived her life according to the ancient teachings in a book which might as well have been labeled fantasy.

*Maybe this is just some weird mid-life crisis coming early.*

Pity party over, Anthony walked inside the dark house.

He heard the murmur of the bedroom television down the hall. Becky was likely watching a recorded chapter of Grey's Anatomy or something.

The only illumination came from the night light along the stairway leading to Ben's room on the second floor.

Looking around in the darkness, Anthony realized he would have been perfectly happy staying at *The Rat's Nest.*

He was a big boy.

He could face the argument and Becky's silent treatment.

Anthony sucked in breath. Whom was he kidding?

He headed towards the warm and familiar and

predictable bedroom.

*Blessed*, Anthony thought with bitterness. *Yeah right.*

## CHAPTER 2

The next morning Anthony woke to the sound of Ben's shuffling footsteps overhead. The boy was like clockwork. With no school on Saturday or Sunday morning, he never came downstairs until the Iron Man clock on his bedside table read 8:00 o'clock.

Crash!

From the sound of it, his son was playing with his Legos and had dropped them all over the hard wood floor.

The bed vibrated as Anthony began to chuckle. He rolled over and touched Becky's forearm. "Looks like our little slugger is up," he whispered.

Becky slid out of the queen-size bed, running a hand lovingly along Anthony's chest as she did so.

He grinned, enjoying the truce that always came with morning. He playfully grabbed at her hand, tempted to yank her back down for some cuddle time. Why not make use of the twenty minutes or so they had before Ben arrived downstairs wanting breakfast.

The idea of a few blissful moments seemed appealing, but the thought didn't last. His arm flopped back onto the bed. Anthony was just too tired. Or maybe it was the depression he didn't know how to shake.

At least he'd cut himself off early enough last night to prevent a hangover, but the taste still lingered in his mouth. Becky probably wouldn't be impressed with his beer breath.

And anyway, she was out of the room before he'd managed to sit up and brush his hair out of his eyes.

The clatter of breakfast preparations was music to his ears as Anthony headed for the bathroom to brush his teeth.

He dressed for the day, pulled up the sheets and the coral bedspread before he moved toward the kitchen to do his part with the meal.

"You okay?" Becky asked as he put the filter into the coffee maker. She'd left her long black hair down the way he liked it.

"Yeah." He wasn't much of a cook and appreciated the fact that Becky enjoyed it. He helped out by setting the table and fixing the coffee in the morning. "Just a little groggy."

"You might consider—" Her dark eyes flashed. And the tone of her voice indicated he wasn't going to like what was about to come out of her mouth. "Staying home on Saturday nights every now and then. I'd like your company, and it just might help you from being so tired and draggy on Sunday mornings."

"Maybe." Anthony shrugged. "But you know the kind of work week I have. I need the time to de-stress and unwind. And before you ask—yes, I know how selfish that sounds."

"Give me two Saturdays in a row," she wheedled. "That's all I'm asking. I'd like to actually *see* my husband every now and then."

"And what would we do, Becky?" he asked gently.

"Rent a movie we both want to see. Remember how we used to snuggle on the couch and watch TV?"

*Did he remember?* Anthony smiled and reached for her.

"And how long has it been since we've had a really good and satisfying talk?" Becky continued. "We used to discuss things for hours when we were dating. Or, God forbid, we could actually be intimate like a husband and wife should be."

Anthony flinched. The words stung, and he knew it was because they were true. He finished setting the table while he let the words sink in and then left the kitchen with the coffee maker percolating behind him.

She sighed in frustration as he passed her, but he paid her no mind. After all, he gave Becky and Ben the whole day on Sunday.

He walked into the bedroom, sat down on their beautiful bed in the tastefully decorated room and checked his phone for work e-mails.

As the senior partner at Dickerson, Markson, & Clark, one of the quickest growing law firms in the city, he had to keep up with the business.

This morning there were six messages waiting for him. E-mails that had not been there at six o' clock yesterday evening. He scanned them quickly and decided they could all wait until tomorrow morning. Becky should be happy about that.

As he set the phone down, he heard the familiar beep that indicated a text message. He checked and saw it was from Janet.

*Maybe next week.*

She never let up. "Don't count on it," Anthony said out loud.

The thunderous footfalls of Ben announced he was coming down to breakfast. *How could such a small boy make so much noise?*

Anthony headed back to the kitchen. No matter how depressed, confused, and bored he was, he couldn't help but smile when he remembered Ben's excitement for today's baseball game.

Although Anthony had no desire to attend, he'd do it because his son wanted to.

His own dad had been a dead-beat who had walked out when Anthony was fourteen, leaving his mother to raise him and his sister, Janet. He wasn't going to be like that with Ben or any other kids he and Becky might have.

Sure, there were lots of things about the current state of his life that he'd like to change, but being a father was something he was proud of. Besides, they'd had to wait six years before Becky had gotten pregnant with Ben.

By the time Anthony joined his family in the kitchen, his son was already at the table. Ben's Yankees baseball cap perched low on his head and covered most of his brown hair.

Ben shoveled in a mouthful of scrambled eggs.

Anthony reached over and tugged the bill of his son's baseball cap lower on his forehead. "Excited about the game, slugger?"

"Yeah." A bit of egg flew out of the child's mouth as he spoke.

"Me, too." Anthony grinned. "Finish up breakfast, and maybe we can head out a little early and watch the team file in."

"Awesome."

Seeing the surprised look Becky gave him, Anthony shrugged. Feeling a twinge of guilt, he walked over and wrapped his arms around her. She laid her head against his chest, and he rested his chin on the top of her head for a moment.

What was he in such a funk about? It certainly wasn't her fault. Anthony knew he had a good life, with a wife who loved him, a son who adored him, a good job, and a beautiful house.

Why did he feel as if he was missing something? Why did he try to numb himself with nights out at places like *The Rat's Nest bar*?

He wasn't sure. And as he stood in the kitchen

with his family, the day rolled out before them, sunny and filled with promise.

So it was hard to come up with an answer.

~*~

With the expanse of outfield laid out in pristine green and the crack of a fastball striking a bat, Anthony found it hard to believe he could be happy anywhere else—not at work, not at a bar, and certainly not at church, as Janet would have argued.

Something about being at the ballpark on a Sunday afternoon helped wash away all of the depression and confusion Anthony had felt earlier.

By the bottom of the third, Ben was ecstatic. Anthony and Becky had to keep reminding him there were other people behind him, trying to see the game.

"Sit down slugger," Anthony cautioned him.

Becky latched onto Ben's shirt. "Stay in your seat and stop jumping up and down."

Still, the weather was gorgeous, his son was having the time of his life, and Anthony and Becky were enjoying the time together. At least he was.

He glanced at Becky. She looked very content. Something he'd not seen in her in quite some time. And she didn't even like most sports.

He wondered again if he was spending too many late nights at work. More than that, maybe he *should* be staying at home on Saturday nights.

He loved Becky. He knew this without a doubt.

But he had no idea why it was so hard to *act* like it. Was it really so difficult to sit with her and listen about her day?

Seriously, would it kill him to stay at home on a Saturday night and watch a movie with her? Maybe a cuddle on the couch *would* be better than numbing his brain with alcohol.

By the time the game was over, Anthony and Becky were holding hands. The little family made their way down the stairs and through the aisles.

Anthony also took Ben's hand as they made their way out of the stadium to the crowded parking lot. He couldn't remember the last time he'd actually felt they were a family—three people living together, loving each other, and relying on one another.

And whose fault was it? He felt stupid for wasting so much of his time at *The Rat's Nest Bar.* What sort of husband was he? What sort of father?

He carefully drove his Porsche through the lot, trying to find a way through the thick traffic heading out after the game.

"You okay?" Becky asked him as he merged into the lane that would take them to the road.

"Yeah. Why?"

She shrugged and gave him a smile. "You seem to be deep in thought about something."

"Not really." He reached out and gave her hand a squeeze. "I just want to apologize for not being home last night. I was being selfish, and I'm sorry."

The comment seemed to take Becky by surprise. But after a moment she returned the loving gesture by gripping his hand. "Thank you."

Still, some part of Anthony wondered if this sense of bliss might be erased tomorrow when he returned to work.

After two or three days of his high stress job, he'd likely feel the need to drink again and start looking forward to a trip to *The Rat's Nest.*

It was always like that. It's just how his brain seemed to work. *But what if I made sure it didn't happen? What if I put the needs of my family first instead of being selfish?*

"Hey, Dad?"

"Yeah, bud?" Anthony glanced at his son in the rearview mirror. The kid was obviously tired, his Yankees cap pulled down low to shade his tired eyes.

"Can we stop for ice cream on the way home?"

Anthony glanced toward Becky to see if he could discern her thoughts. Still mellow from the day, she gave a cute little shrug and played with her hair.

"Okay," Anthony said. "Since Mom is agreeable, I don't see why not."

Ben perked up, excited all over again.

*One thing for sure—the kid was going to sleep good tonight.*

Becky trailed her fingers along his thigh. "This was nice. We should do this again."

"We should." Anthony grinned. Becky had always hated baseball.

He drove onto the expressway and headed home.

The city fell away behind them, and Anthony wound into the suburbs where they lived. He was truly lucky to have his life. He was sure Janet would not call it *lucky*. No, she would call it *blessed*.

And maybe that *was* what it was called. But if he was blest with such a great family, he had no idea what he had ever done to deserve them. If there *was* a God, as Janet believed, and if He was in control of the show, then He apparently just handed out great lives to undeserving people.

Anthony didn't get it. He'd take it, but he sure didn't get it.

He had made mistakes in the past, and any sufficient God would not have rewarded him with such an amazing family and a great life.

So even if there *was* a God, He seemed to be sort of lenient.

Then Anthony smirked. *Now that is a God I could get behind.*

## CHAPTER 3

At exactly 6:30 on Monday morning, Anthony and Becky exchanged their normal quick and hasty good-bye kiss.

He sprinted out the front door—and was soon behind the wheel of his Porsche—headed for work.

It was odd, but the car felt different than it had on the way home from the ballgame yesterday. No longer filled with the joy and promise of happy days ahead for him and his family, now the vehicle was nothing more than the set of wheels designed to carry him to his office.

Anthony always showed up early to knock out responses to weekend e-mails so he could get them out of the way and dig into his *real* morning work.

The Monday after taking Ben to the ballgame was no different.

He liked his job and got an almost excessive amount of fulfillment out of it. The plush office, the perks, and prestige of finally becoming senior partner were gratifying. But he knew without a doubt his workaholic tendencies were turning him into a miserable human being.

Anthony helped people with personal injury issues. And he had at least one client who was simply trying to milk people with undue or unjust claims.

By the very nature of the job, the hours were long, and the work itself was stressful. In fact, the majority of his co-workers were unhappy and negative people.

This was never more apparent than on Monday mornings.

Anthony was busy returning messages from clients and his fellow partners in the firm, when the other office employees started to funnel in.

Within minutes, he heard voices laced with anger, frustration, and overall contempt.

He'd known working as an attorney would be stressful and, at times, emotional. But it was Anthony's job to represent those people.

The money was very good, he'd admit. Still, he saw the lower side of the human race several times a week. The most pathetic part of it all was that in order to do his job properly, he sometimes had to stoop to their level.

No wonder his gut ached. Could that be the major source of his depression?

Taking no more time to dwell on himself, Anthony was on the phone most of the day, speaking with clients, and putting out fires. He even had to cancel lunch with a high-roller due to an emergency with another couple and their accumulating medical bills.

By the time 2:00 o' clock rolled around, Anthony was exhausted. He had no idea how he would make it through the rest of the week. The fact was he was hungry, fatigued, bored, and disconnected from everything.

He pictured the bright green expanse of outfield he'd seen yesterday and remembered the sparkle in Ben's eyes. Things had simply seemed *right* on the way home. Maybe it was time to buy a season pass to the games.

But more than anything, Anthony could still see the look of shock on Becky's face when he had apologized for being selfish.

Why had she been so surprised? Did she really receive so few kind words from him that when she *did* hear them it was like some miraculous occurrence?

Before the clock hit 2:30, Anthony had had enough. Even though he had two more calls and a face-to-face meeting later in the day, his office girl could reschedule all of that.

He got up from his desk and headed to the reception area in the front.

Miranda looked at him through her horn rimmed glasses with the same sort of tired smile everyone else at the firm seemed to wear. The sparkle had left her eyes long ago.

"I'm heading out for the day," he told the receptionist.

# Awareness

"You feel okay?"

Anthony paused to think about this. He *did* feel okay, but something seemed not quite right. And perhaps that was why he was leaving early.

He forced a smile. "Yeah. There's just some family stuff I need to take care of. Could you please contact the rest of my appointments for this afternoon and reschedule?"

Miranda pushed her glasses up on her nose. "Sure thing."

Anthony turned and headed out the front doors. When he stepped into the afternoon sunshine, he sensed a glimmer of the same hope and promise he'd felt after the baseball game yesterday afternoon. Maybe he could hold onto it for the rest of the day.

His steps were lighter as he walked to his Porsche, and he had no idea why. But he made several decisions as he got into the car.

For one thing, he was going to cook the evening meal so Becky wouldn't have to worry with it when she got off work. In fact he'd impress her with a full course Latino meal. Just because he was blond didn't mean he didn't appreciate her heritage.

And after dinner, he was going to toss the baseball around with Ben in the backyard.

But before all of that, he was going to pick up a simple little present for Becky.

It was about time he put his family first and his

own needs—especially his career—second.

And oddly enough, he couldn't wait to get started.

Becky had few guilty pleasures, but one of them was the strawberry-sprinkled vanilla ice cream bars that she'd only been able to find in a little convenience store twelve blocks away from their house.

She'd eaten tons of them in college and during their courtship and engagement. The days, she'd mentioned, when they'd spent hours discussing issues they were both interested in.

Even during the early years of their marriage, they'd go by *Sam and Ethel's* convenience store and end the night with a strawberry ice cream bar.

He couldn't remember the last time they'd enjoyed one of those bars together, but he was certain it had been at least six years. Ever since they'd had Ben.

In those days he was so delighted with his longed-for son that he buckled down and concentrated on his career so that he would provide for his family. He would gaze at the photo of Becky holding their little slugger on her lap. His Mexican-heritage queen and their beautifully blended boy. It gave him energy to deal with the darker side of the business. When did that change?

He needed to return to some of the simple pleasures Becky and he used to enjoy. He wanted to see her smile when he presented her with the frozen treat from the past.

Memories tumbled back as he parked the car in the store's lot. The building itself looked exactly the same, and although he knew there was no guarantee that they still carried Becky's ice cream of choice, he had a good feeling as he walked through the sliding doors with a bounce in his step.

The place was situated along the border of the part of the city that some might call the *wrong side of town.* Another hole in the wall. But he had to admit the atmosphere was better than *The Rat's Nest.*

Being 3:30 in the afternoon, he found the place practically dead. One lone customer scoured the beer cooler while the cashier sat behind the counter, watching a court show on TV.

Anthony spotted the ice cream box, still located where it had been all those years ago, and grinned as he approached it.

When he looked inside and saw the familiar white and pink wrapping, he let out a chuckle.

He slid the door open and reached inside. He grabbed two, then three, before he put them back into the box and took the entire thing out.

Feeling slightly silly, Anthony made his way to the counter and set the box down. He'd never been able to purchase a whole box in those early days. In fact some weeks he and Becky had to share one.

A small rack standing by the counter was haphazardly filled with sloppily wrapped flower assortments. They weren't the prettiest things, but they seemed to bring back more memories. If he trimmed them up a bit and put them in one of Becky's vases, they could look nice.

On an impulse, he picked up the nicest bouquet he could find and placed it by his box of ice cream.

"Ice cream and flowers? What did you do to get in so much trouble?" the cashier asked with smirk as he counted the number of ice cream bars.

"No trouble." Anthony puffed out his chest. "Just trying to finally do the right thing."

The man nodded as he finished counting. "That's eleven bars?"

Anthony nodded.

"That'll be twenty-four dollars and eighteen cents."

As Anthony handed over his credit card, a barely perceptible movement indicated another customer had come into the store.

The cashier slid Anthony's card through the credit card machine, paused a beat, and then reached Anthony's card across to him.

Before Anthony could take it, the cashier dropped the card on the counter, his eyes suddenly wide and afraid.

It was pure instinct that moved Anthony to look behind him.

# Awareness

The barrel of a gun stood less than six inches from his forehead. Out of focus from Anthony's eyes which locked onto the barrel of the gun, was the blurred silhouette of a man in a ski-mask.

"On the floor."

Frozen with fear, Anthony couldn't respond, his brain still shooting up a million red flags at the sight of the gun.

"I said *get on the floor.*"

At last, Anthony's body caught up with his panicked mind. He raised his hands at the same moment as he lowered himself to his knees. He then awkwardly lowered his body to lie on his stomach.

"Don't look up." The masked man walked past Anthony and approached the register. "And *you,*" he said. "Give me the money that's in the cash drawer and the safe."

"Yeah," the cashier said. "Just be cool, okay? Be cool and—"

That's when the man who'd been searching the beer aisle came walking to the register. He'd obviously been so preoccupied with his selection that he didn't see the gunman.

The man in the mask wheeled, stepped toward him and yelled. *"On the floor, now."*

The customer dropped the package to the floor. The clinking of breaking bottles was followed by the fizzing sound of released beer.

As Anthony raised his head, the masked man

turned back toward the cashier, the gunman's eyes widened as the cashier's had been earlier. Obviously something was not going according to plan.

But before Anthony could put it all together, a gunshot rang out.

# CHAPTER 4

Everything appeared to be happening on a time delay—as if the world had skipped a beat, and was now catching up with itself.

From his position on the floor, Anthony watched the would-be robber's feet stumble backwards.

Anthony was quite sure the shot had been fired by the cashier. Likely he'd had a gun stashed behind the counter, and the customer with the beer was a distraction of which the cashier had been able to take advantage.

As a hole appeared in the white shirt the gunman wore, Anthony raised his head a bit more. The hole filled in with dark red. TV apparently got it wrong when it came to the shade of blood-red.

The gun wobbled in the wounded man's hand but he managed to raise it again. However, before he could pull the trigger, the cashier let off another round.

A second hole appeared directly in the center of the robber's chest, and he stumbled to one knee. The eyes behind the ski mask appeared blank and defeated, but the man still managed to fire a shot.

Anthony could actually *feel* the sound as well as hear it. He'd heard about these gun fights but had never witnessed one. Would the experience make him a better lawyer?

The first shot plowed into the plywood face of the counter, sending splinters of wood into his hair.

He jerked as the second shot hit a little lower and more splinters targeted him. Anthony heard another blast of the gun but no sound of the hit.

Another blast, and then another, exploded the air nearby. But there was no other noise. No plywood target splintering with the shock of another bullet piercing its layers.

Only a heavy pinching sensation just below his left shoulder. Confusion and then a growing pain between his shoulder and breastbone eventually penetrated his brain.

Insurmountable agony surged through his body. He lowered his head to the floor once more and opened his mouth to scream, but no sound came out.

The floor vibrated, and he was dimly aware the robber had fallen close by. Anthony let out a gasp. The pain seemed to escape through his mouth, but the noise barely sounded human.

*This is not good. Oh my God, I've been shot.*

He moaned and tried to rise to his knees. The pain slammed his chest. He gasped for breath as he lowered his self again. The taste of blood filled his mouth.

A flurry of motion came from his right side, but

he was afraid to move to check it out—afraid the pain would increase, afraid he wasn't man enough to handle it.

*Was the shooter back on his feet and coming to finish the job?* Maybe this time he'd put the gun directly against Anthony's skull. Maybe that would be a relief.

"Hang on, Mister."

Anthony blinked and relaxed as he recognized the cashier leaning over him, wide-eyed and pale.

"Shot." Anthony breathed.

"Yeah. He got you pretty good. Hang in there, okay? I'm calling 9-1-1."

Anthony couldn't say more, so he blinked his eyes. He still tasted blood in his mouth, and now he could feel liquid thickness cascade down his chest.

Before he choked on his own blood, he mouthed the only words that came to his pain-stricken mind. "The ice-cream. Don't let it melt."

"Yeah, yeah." The cashier absently punched numbers into his phone.

Anthony looked at the shooter, the gun still clutched in his motionless hand. Roughly, three feet separated them, and Anthony couldn't help but wonder if the man was dead.

And if the robber was dead, how much longer would it be before Anthony followed? The pain continued to radiate outward as he heard the cashier speak into the phone.

Anthony felt woozy, and a peculiar numbness began to bloom along his left side. He tried shifting his left arm and hand. It moved a little. But he couldn't feel it. It was as if he was watching the limb of someone else.

Suddenly, the cashier was beside him again. "Hang in there. An ambulance is on the way. Hang in there, man."

Anthony didn't have the strength to acknowledge him, or do anything to help himself.

Evidently he'd rolled on his back in his anguish, and he gazed at the ceiling. His mind conjured up a picture of Ben and Becky at the baseball game He saw again, the perfect green of the outfield.

*Put the ice cream back in the box. Don't let it melt. Becky can use it to remember me by.* He rolled his eyes towards the counter as the almost hysterical thought came again.

Then his body started to pull away—to give up on him. He felt a sense movement. This was odd. He was quite certain he was still lying on the floor of Sam and Ethel's convenience store. Lying in a pool of his own blood. But he felt a sense of motion, as if he were a leaf caught in a fall breeze.

He got the distinct impression that if he simply followed the breeze and snuggled deeper into the darkness, the pain from the gunshot would be gone, as would the floor beneath him and the panicked storeowner who was still hunkered down over him, speaking words Anthony couldn't understand.

But then the shadowy darkness morphed into an expanse of green so bright his eyes hurt.

He was at the outfield at Yankee Stadium, sitting in the stands. The stadium was deserted, and he was all alone.

An absolute silence filled the world.

And then the soft *slap* of a baseball meeting a glove broke the quiet.

Anthony looked down onto the outfield, expecting to see himself and Ben throwing the ball. Instead, he saw a much younger version of himself throwing a baseball with his father.

"Dad." Young Anthony's voice was like a lost breeze in a forest.

His dad had come back into his life when he'd graduated from college, but had died eight years ago of pancreatic cancer. Yet when Anthony spoke his name, the much younger version of his father looked up into the stands and smiled. The child-version of Anthony seemed oblivious and stared out into the huge world of green.

"There's nothing for you past here," his dad said. "You head on back now, Anthony. Your family needs you."

Anthony wanted to say something—something he wished he'd done before his father had passed away—but the darkness shifted, and Anthony became aware of several sets of hands touching him.

When he opened his eyes, three faces looked down on him. The convenience store ceiling was hazy beyond their heads.

With hands hooked beneath him, the men began to lift Anthony. The pain was so great he would have screamed if he could open his mouth. But now, even that was too much of an effort.

The men set him on something—a stretcher, he assumed—and he felt the sensation of movement again. He closed his eyes against the dizziness.

He could sense when they reached the outside, and Anthony opened his eyes to the red swirling lights of an ambulance.

With a lift and a shove, his stretcher was in the back, and the ambulance door slammed. Two medics in the back of the vehicle began to speak.

The sirens roar sounded far away. After a while it became as faint as birdsong, and Anthony revisited the darkness.

Again, he sensed the expanse of green waiting for him, but figured it might be best to heed his father's advice and stay away.

He willed himself to focus and stay anchored to the real world. *If I go to it again, I won't wake up. I won't open my eyes again. It is death. That field is death.*

Although in a sort of twilight, Anthony caught the occasional words of the men in the ambulance. *Blood loss, critical, bleed out,* and others even more terrifying.

The ambulance stopped, and the doors opened filling the interior of the ambulance with fresh air.

The stretcher was moved again, and when the medics set him down outside, the wheels squeaked beneath him.

With an eerie sort of grace, the stretcher glided along the path, and Anthony once again felt like a leaf in the wind. He kept his eyes closed, as the constant movement nauseated him.

He sensed a whole new sort of darkness coming on, but this one seemed safe. Nothing more than the darkness of rest, and he let himself drift into it.

"Your driver's license says you're Anthony Markson. Can you hear me, Anthony?"

He roused enough to mouth *yes*, but he kept his eyes shut. *How would Becky and Ben take the news of his injuries?*

Then he relaxed, and embraced the peaceful darkness.

## CHAPTER 5

"Anthony? Anthony, sweetheart, can you hear me?"

Becky's brown face hovered inches from his own. The relief surging through him was immense, but still not quite strong enough to drown out the crushing pain that barreled through him.

An anvil sat on top of his chest, and every muscle in his body throbbed as if he had just run a marathon. The vise attached to his head kept tightening.

"Becky." he breathed.

"Thank God, you're okay." She leaned forward and kissed him softly, as if she was afraid he might break.

"How long have I been here?" The intense pain grounded him—helped him forget the leaf he'd seen shifting in the breeze.

"Fifteen hours. They took you right back to surgery when you arrived. Thankfully, it went smoothly."

"I was shot," he whispered. Knowing a bullet had penetrated his body sobered him. He lacked the strength to even cry.

"I know."

He glanced around at the generic hospital room,

fear and safety tugging at his emotions. "Ben?" he asked.

Becky grabbed his hand "He's at the neighbor's house. I'll call them with an update when the doctor gets in."

As his Caucasian fingers interlocked with her Hispanic ones, Anthony choked up. He wished Becky could have seen the green outfield from when he had slipped away. He found himself wanting to apologize for so many different things.

"I knew you'd want Janet to know you were here," Becky said as she squeezed his hand. "I called her right away."

"Thanks."

"I've been keeping her up to date. When you came out of surgery two hours ago, she indicated she'd be here sometime tonight."

Anthony agonized over the many texts he'd received from Janet and how he'd ignored most of them. If he had died after the gunshot, those unanswered texts would be his last impression on his sister.

Pathetic when you considered how she had rallied around when their mother died while he was still in college. No wonder Janet continued to *mother* him.

He glanced at Becky. She'd been crying and looked very tired. *Had she been awake all night?*

"You know," he said, hoping to lift her spirits. "I

went to *Sam and Ethel's* store to get some ice cream bars. The strawberry ones you enjoyed so well."

"I figured as much. Much as I like them, they are not worth this."

"I don't know about that." The chuckle that rose from his throat hurt his chest. He swallowed. "You're worth—"

At a gentle knock on the door, they turned to see a cheerful-looking doctor come into the room carrying a clipboard and a folder.

"Good to see you're awake. How are you feeling?"

"Sore," Anthony said. "Tired."

"You can add *lucky* to the list." The doctor moved to the edge of the bed and stood beside Becky. "We were able to remove the bullet and repair the damage. But if that slug had been a half inch lower, the chances of your survival would have been slim to none."

Anthony clutched Becky's hand while he searched the doctor's face. "But I'm going to be okay?"

"You'll remain sore for a few days, and the injury will itch unbearably while it heals. But yes, outside of keeping you here a while longer for observation, it seems you're out of the woods."

The doctor checked the monitors. Then he ran a series of cognitive tests, checked Anthony's vision, and reflexes.

"Looking good." The doctor gave a smile of

approval. "A nurse will check back in an hour or so. I suggest you get some rest. Right now, it's the best thing for your body."

"I'll try," Anthony said. "Thanks."

A very relieved looking Becky smiled at the doctor. "Yes, doctor. Thanks *so* much."

"One more thing. Don't be surprised if you find yourself crying more than usual. Any surgery near the heart seems to affect patient's emotions." The doctor turned about and left the room.

Becky's face scrunched. She heaved deeply and wept into the side of Anthony's hospital bed. "I thought I had lost you."

He reached out and stroked her dark hair. "Well you didn't. "I'm still here, and I'm not planning on going anywhere."

Again the picture came to him of playing catch on the outfield with his old man. What did it mean? He sensed there was some great power waiting for him on the other side of the grass.

So was it really something to avoid, or not?

~*~

Taking the doctor's advice and resting was easy because Anthony fell asleep with Becky still clinging to the side of the bed, their hands interlocked.

An hour and a half later, when a nurse came into the room to check on him, he roused. The nurse assured him that his vitals were good and he was headed in the right direction.

He lolled his head back on the pillow but now he was wide awake and too anxious to get back to sleep.

Becky had pulled a chair close to the bed and sat beside him quietly.

He studied her face and wondered what it had been like to receive the phone call letting her know her husband of twelve years had been shot.

How much had she seen? Had she caught a glimpse of him before the surgery, soaked in blood while being pushed on a gurney?

He continued to stare at his wife. She was so beautiful the way her long hair framed her face, and. he was overwhelmed by how much he loved her. Ashamed of how badly he had treated her for most of their marriage, he let a few tears slip out. Things were going to change.

A knock sounded at the door, and Anthony expected it was the doctor or a nurse coming to check on him again. Instead, Janet poked her head around the door. At fifty two, along with her short salt and pepper colored hair, the stress and worry on her face made her look eerily like their mother.

"Come on in." His voice was amazingly weak.

His sister slowly entered the room looking at him as if she didn't trust her own eyes.

Becky rose from the chair with a smile, and the two women met with a hug at the end of the hospital bed.

# Awareness

Janet looked back at her brother over Becky's head and frowned. "Oh, Anthony are you really okay?"

"According to the doctors."

"Am I intruding?" Janet asked, glancing at Becky.

"Of course not." Becky patted the back of the chair where she'd been sitting. "In fact, why don't you stay with him for a while? I need to go find some coffee."

"Coffee sounds good. Could you bring me a cup too?"

With a nod, Becky headed out.

Janet took up the post Becky had previously occupied by the bed. "I don't even know what to say. You are all the family I have left. I was so terrified."

"I was a little scared, too," Anthony admitted with a sheepish laugh.

"I prayed for you the entire way here. I know you don't buy into that, but I did it anyway."

Anthony thought of the green outfield and how their father had spoken to him. "Actually, I appreciate it."

*Maybe, the power I felt on the other side of the grass was God.* It was a jarring thought. Anthony had always believed in a god of some sort, but he had basically ruled out the God who Janet devoted her life to.

Still what or who had directed him back to the world of the living, using the vision of his deceased father?

Anthony had been borderline rude to Janet every time she'd mentioned her faith. Now, as she sat at his bedside while a bandage covered his surgery wound, he wondered just how she had acquired such faith.

More than that, he wondered how *he* could get it. But he immediately put the thought at the back of his mind.

"Whether or not it was your praying that did it," Anthony said offhandedly, "the doctor indicated I was lucky. Half an inch lucky, to be exact."

"Yeah, I know. Becky told me. Would you mind if I pray over you right now?"

Anthony was a bit taken aback. But what harm could there be? "II guess it would be okay."

With a smile on her face, Janet took both of his hands in hers. She clasped them tightly and bowed her head.

"Lord, thank you for saving Anthony. Thank you for your grace and your mercy and thank you for—"

Anthony didn't hear the rest. Out of nowhere, a tremendous flood of grief tore through him, and he wept.

He saw the green outfield again, but this time, his father and his younger self were nowhere to be seen. Instead, it was just him in his current thirty-seven year old body.

*Anthony.* A soft voice penetrated his mind. *I have*

*chosen you. I have work for you to do. But you need to accept and know Me first.*

Then just as quickly it was gone. The voice and the outfield. All gone in the blink of an eye.

When the vision faded, he realized he was still crying, and Janet was holding him close.

"Anthony, what's wrong? Are you okay?"

"I'm sorry."

"What for?" Janet asked.

"I don't know." And he didn't.

He wasn't sure if the apology was directed at Janet, Becky, or God. Maybe it was intended for all three.

"But I--I think I need to talk to you."

"About what?"

He looked at her sheepishly, "God."

## CHAPTER 6

Anthony looked expectantly at his sister. "So, what can you tell me?"

Janet smiled through tear filled eyes. She leaned forward, taking his hand. "I've been praying you'd see one day. That you'd realize there is a God and feel a genuine need for Him."

"I still don't know about any of that," Anthony protested. "But something happened between the time I was shot and my waking up here. Something beautiful and weird at the same time. Something profound and intimate. Something in the darkness between here and death was speaking directly to me."

Janet tilted her head. "And you don't think it was God?"

"I don't know." Anthony shrugged "But whatever it was, it was something I never realized could exist. I have to think it was supernatural. Call it God or whatever you want."

Janet nodded slowly, tears still filling her eyes. "I'd call it God."

A nurse entered the room and seemed to notice Janet's tears. "I need to take Mr. Markson's vitals. Can I get you anything?"

"No, it's okay," Janet said. "Please, come on in."

The nurse moved to Anthony's bedside. "They'll be bringing your dinner up shortly. Of course, there are several things you can't have this soon after your surgery. So, I'll warn you, the fare is going to be pretty meager."

"That's okay. Actually, I'd just like something to drink."

The nurse took his blood pressure. "I'll make a note of that. I think you are on a liquid diet anyway."

Anthony felt the cuff tighten around his forearm and then slack up.

Janet dabbed her eyes with a tissue she'd pulled from her purse.

The nurse finished listing Anthony's vitals and headed out.

The moment she was gone, Anthony turned to his sister. "How can you have such a strong faith? What makes you so sure about God?"

"I just do. I know it's an unsatisfactory answer, but that's the way it is."

"There has to be more to it."

"I gave my life to Christ twelve years ago, about the time you and Becky married."

"But why?"

"Because I felt a prompting. I felt Him tugging at me. And when I surrendered my life, everything else fell into place. After you accept Him, the faith part just sort of works itself out."

"So you're telling me that if I died because of this shooting, your faith wouldn't have been shaken?"

Janet tilted her head and gave a crooked smile, as if amused by the question. "While I would have wondered *why* He decided to take you, leaving behind a wife and young son," she began, "and it's perfectly okay to wonder why things happen, but no, I don't think I would have questioned His decision. I've learned He does all things for good."

"Even in death?"

"Yes." She looked him in the eye. "But He didn't take you. In fact, if what you're saying is true, then I think He might have used this situation to open your eyes to Him. I think He's calling you."

"I didn't see God when I was out cold." His voice mocked her.

"Are you sure? Want to tell me what you did see?"

He was tempted. He really was. But he decided to keep it to himself. For now.

He shook his head. "Maybe some other time." It was too close to him and much too personal to share just yet.

"Fair enough. Whatever God's reasoning, I'm glad you made it through. I love you, Anthony."

"Thanks. I love you, too, sis. According to the doctor, it was *really* close."

"I know. He thought you got lucky, but, I think it might have been something else."

He chuckled, knowing full well where she was

going with this train of thought. "And what might that something else be?"

"It doesn't matter. That's not the important thing."

"Then what is?"

Janet smiled and squeezed his hand. "The important thing is God has chosen you for something special. Whatever you saw or felt, you need to figure that out on your own."

"I'm not sure I know how."

"You need to let it sink in, accept Him and let Him show you what it's all about."

~*~

For the next three days Anthony went over the conversation he and Janet had shared. Each time he rolled it through his mind, an incredible peace settled over him.

It wasn't just the fact he had survived the shooting—he was truly beginning to think that there *was* indeed some sort of purpose for his life.

How many people escaped near-fatal shootings like that and lived to tell about it?

~*~

When Anthony was finally released from the hospital Becky drove him home.

Ben sat in the back seat gaping at his father as if he was some sort of superhero.

Anthony was still sore. When he'd watched the nurse change his bandages, it was hard to discern where the wounds from the bullet hole began and the surgery wound ended.

"You okay?" Becky reached out and patted his hand.

"Yeah, I think so. I'm just glad to be heading back home. A hospital is not a place to rest."

Becky laughed. "I have strict instructions from the doctor, and I'm warning you now. You will be resting on my watch."

The neighborhood rolled by as they headed home. The soft pitter patter of raindrops on the window soothed Anthony's emotions, surrounding him with a peaceful drowsiness.

When they pulled into the garage, Ben was eager to help his dad get out of the car and walk into the house. Anthony didn't think he needed the assistance, but he wanted his son to feel like he was contributing. What he could hardly accept was the look of reverence and awe in his son's eyes.

Anthony had been neglectful of the important things and had a lot to make up for.

"Okay, doctor's orders." Becky smacked Anthony playfully on his backside. "Get your butt in bed and sleep."

"If you insist." Anthony gave a manly protest. In reality he was thankful for her orders. He *was* very tired.

Becky nodded. "Meanwhile I'll make something healthy for dinner to make sure you bounce back quickly."

Entering the bedroom with a woozy head and a sore body, Anthony gratefully pulled back the coral sheets, and lay down.

He couldn't help but think about his shaky relationship with God as he mulled over the conversation he'd shared with Janet in the hospital. He'd never, *not* believed in God, but he also had never come close to being the Holy Roller his sister was.

He didn't really know why, but the people she worshiped with had always infuriated him. Since they repelled him, he'd wanted nothing to do with church or interacting with God.

Anthony had always assumed his belief in God—as vague and undefined as it was—would be enough for his salvation.

He had his ticket to Heaven, and that was enough. Wasn't it?

But after surviving the shooting, he couldn't help but wonder if there was something more for him. And if that was true, perhaps there was more to God than he'd thought.

Anthony looked back over his life, trying to analyze where he'd always stood with the Lord.

He vaguely remembered Sunday school as a kid. Then he and Becky had gone to church a handful of times after getting married, simply because it had felt like the right thing to do.

So he had always *sort of* known there was God. But had he really cared?

Anthony lifted his shirt up to examine his wounds. Of course, they were still bandaged, but as he ran his hands over them, he considered the fragility of his life.

*I should be dead. Even the doctors were awed how I managed to make it through.*

Quietly and carefully, Anthony got out of bed and crossed to the small bookshelf on the other side of the bed. He had to scan through the titles before locating the Bible. He couldn't remember the last time it had been taken down.

He took the Bible back to bed with him. After taking some time to comfortably situate the pillows behind him so as not to aggravate his wounds, he opened the book at random and smirked. *If only Janet could see me now.*

He scanned a few lines and came to a section of Psalms that reached up and slapped him hard across the face. "My flesh and my heart may fail, but God is the strength of my heart and my portion forever."

*My heart may fail*

Tears fell, and he had no idea where they were coming from.

He read Psalm 73:26 again, and this time he felt a warming in his ear which seemed to radiate through his entire body.

*My heart may fail*

## Awareness

He chuckled a bit. He had to in order to keep more tears away.

"Okay, God." He looked skyward with purpose. Something he'd not done in a very long time. "You've got my attention. Now what?"

## CHAPTER 7

Anthony had spent the past two weeks resting in bed and reading more and more scripture.

He'd kept the Bible on his bedside table, and the majority of what he read was familiar echoes of things he'd learned while in Sunday school, or during the few times he'd sat in church as an adult.

But as he continued to read, the chapters he perused began to have a spark in them. The words became alive and active, and passages seemed to speak as if written just for him.

He had never considered contact with God could only be concocted by a fanatical imagination. Or that only crazy people thought they had contact with some divine being.

No, even as a shaky believer, he'd known that having God speak to you was more about movement in your heart than an actual audible conversation. And now he felt God continually nudging him in some subtle and not-so-subtle ways since he had arrived home.

At first, Anthony tried to tell himself it was really nothing more than narrowly dodging death and having an entirely new appreciation for life. But there were far too many things to consider. And they couldn't all be coincidences. Because every bit of scripture he'd read since returning home had spoken directly to him in some way or another.

Beyond that, he was learning a very important lesson. All throughout the Bible, God chose to work through people who did not know Him at first.

It was strange, but God didn't often pick people who had been long-time devoted followers. Rather, the opposite was true. God seemed to call those far removed from Him, those who lived in sin with tumultuous and often deplorable lives.

This reminded Anthony of the old saying, "Don't call me, I'll call you."

While Anthony didn't think he was on par with some of the hard-cases God had worked with in the Bible, he also knew he was the furthest thing from a saint.

Something about seeing the nature and aims of God in such a way seemed inescapable.

He had no idea where the idea came from, but every time he opened the Bible, Anthony felt as if he was being prepared for something.

And that *something* was more than just being bowled over by scripture on a personal level. He had no idea what it might be, and it weighed heavily on him.

He couldn't find the courage to mention it to Becky. Still, he knew as his wife, she would pick up on it anyway.

On several different occasions, he nearly called Janet. He wanted to ask her what it was like to actually feel the presence of God. What was it like to have God speak to you?

But she'd told him he had to figure this one out on his own. And besides, it was all pretty new and precious.

So on this, the fourteenth day since he'd been released from the hospital, Becky was busy fixing grilled chicken with a garden salad.

As she had promised, they were making an effort to eat healthy while Anthony got his strength back.

"You've been reading the Bible a lot lately. Are you rediscovering the purpose of life after nearly losing it?" The tone of Becky's voice indicated her words were intended to be a joke, but there also seemed to be a bit of hope behind them.

"Something like that. I think. I'm about positive there might be some reasons I survived."

She leaned toward him with a smile. "Of course there was. Ben and I need you."

"Yes, but I also think God has some sort of a plan for me."

The room was quiet after this comment, and Anthony saw a slight smile touch Becky's face. Ben, however, frowned as he pushed his chicken around with his fork.

"Does this mean we're going to have to start going to church?" Ben asked in a disappointed whine.

Anthony chuckled. "It just might."

They finished dinner without much conversation. Ben appeared to be brooding about a test he had the following day. At least he was awfully quiet.

Anthony wondered, though, if some of Ben's mood might be coming from the fact he'd almost lost his father not so long ago.

It was still two hours before Anthony normally settled down, but on this night he retired to bed at 8:30.

When Becky came into the room an hour later he woke for a few moments, and images of the man with the gun and the sounds of gunshots in the convenience store filled his mind.

As he drifted off to sleep again, the gun lingered large in his consciousness.

And that's when the dream began.

Being aware it was a dream made the experience all the more surreal, but Anthony allowed it to carry him forward. He was powerless to do anything about it anyway.

Once again he found himself in a large green outfield, the same one he and his family had been sitting behind during the baseball game a little more than three weeks ago. This time he was alone, although there was a cross standing in the infield, directly where second base should have been.

Anthony limped towards the cross, as if he didn't

quite trust it.

He glanced toward the empty stands. In fact, there was not a single soul in the ballpark. Just him.

Grey thunderheads rolled in, covering up the blue sky. Anthony again glanced toward the cross and realized he'd traveled further than he'd expected and was now standing in front of it.

He had moved with dreamlike quality, as if it had pulled him to it like a magnetic force. And he sensed there was something sacred about the cross. It was easily twelve feet tall, its horizontal arms reaching out a good eight feet in both directions.

Thinking of references in scripture where people reacted to sacred ground, Anthony kicked off his shoes and slowly bent his knees until they touched the turf. He then lowered himself even further, placing his forehead to the ground and clasping his hands in prayer.

"Lord, I'm so sorry. I know I've forgotten you. I know I've sinned against you. And still, you spared my life. Tell me what you want from me, and you'll have it."

"It's not what I want." A voice from behind him startled Anthony. "But what you are willing to offer."

With pounding heart Anthony rose from his prone position and wheeled around, expecting to see the celestial face of the almighty.

Instead, he saw the masked face of the man in the

*Sam and Ethel's* store. He held no gun this time, but a baseball, which he tossed playfully from one hand to the other.

Confusion filled Anthony's mind. This man being here made no sense.

The image of the man who had nearly killed him three weeks ago smiled. "No man shall see the true face of God and live."

An undeniable peace and calm radiated through Anthony as the man spoke. *Well, it's no burning bush. But it certainly gets my attention.*

"There are others like you," the man continued. "You are all my children but have fallen away. You have all lived through traumas because I have spared you from death. And the reason I spared you from death is so you can go out and do my work."

"What work?" Anthony croaked.

"Pay attention." The man took a step closer. "Pay attention and it will become clear to you."

Anthony tried to focus on the man, but the sun shone directly through his face, not allowing him to get a clear view.

"There will be signs and miracles set forth for you," the man continued. "I want you to travel to the others and help them. You are my chosen people, and there is a great need for the gifts that I will grant to each of you."

Anthony absorbed the message, but could not find any words to reply.

"Will you go?"

"I will," Anthony said.

"Now look at me, my son."

Anthony looked up, aware of the tears in his eyes. What he saw was not the face of God at all, but looked more like the sun. But from inside the sun, a hand reached out to him.

It was in that moment Anthony woke up. He sat bolt upright in bed, heart pounding, drenched in sweat, and gasping for breath.

He couldn't figure out why the man with the gun had represented God in this dream. But once the significance of the dream itself sank into him, the fear morphed into something bordering on joy. He smiled and wept softly.

Becky slowly sat up beside him. "Are you okay?"

"Yes," he said into the darkness of the bedroom.

"You have a bad dream or something?"

"Not exactly. No, not a bad one at all." And then he couldn't help himself. He started laughing joyously.

God had spoken to Anthony. He had been *selected* by a God he had scarcely even believed in until a few weeks ago.

The experience deserved praise but the best he could do in that moment was to laugh.

# CHAPTER 8

It was just after 6:00 o'clock in the morning, and Ben was upstairs getting ready for school when Anthony called his sister. He knew she was an early bird, and he was also well aware of Becky's dark eyes glancing over at him.

Anthony figured his wife knew something was different about him. She was like that. But they'd had no real time to discuss it. Not before he called Janet.

His hand shook as he held the phone, waiting for his sister to pick up. Getting ready for work, no doubt, or she would have snatched it up after the first ring. As it was, the phone rang twice before he heard her voice.

"Hello?"

"Hey Janet. It's your big brother." He hated to bother her, but he really needed to talk to her.

She was silent for a moment, probably adding up his call, the early hour, and assuming something was wrong. "You mean my six foot tall baby brother. Is everything okay?"

"Absolutely. But that's six foot two, I'll have you know."

"Whatever. Are you healing up okay?" Her voice

was cautious.

"Yes, Janet. I'm fine. But I was wondering if there was any way I could speak with you today. Maybe I could come have lunch with you."

Again, a brief silence. "Sounds good. Are you? Um."

"What?"

"Okay," she continued. "I'm just going to say it."

"Say what?"

She sighed. "If you hang up, I'll understand. But, Anthony, I've been praying for you ever since you asked me about God in the hospital. Well, I've always prayed. But this time I've been praying *nonstop.* And one of my prayers last night was that God would talk to you. That He would be bold and apparent because you're so stubborn. You know you are. But anyway I got this sense of peace. It's like He told me everything was going to be okay."

Tears welled up in his eyes as he listened on the phone. "I think you're right."

He held out his hand towards Becky, and she took it with a tentative smile and wide eyes. *Could she tell that something spectacular was taking place?*

"Janet, is it too much to ask if I can see you soon? How about meeting for breakfast?"

"It happened, didn't it? Anthony, tell me what happened."

"Last night I had a dream. A *vision* maybe. No burning bushes or anything like that, but He was, as you put it, bold and apparent."

Anthony heard a gasp on the other end. He could recognize Janet's weeping anywhere because she tended to cry quite a lot—happy, sad, whatever.

"Yes," she croaked. "Breakfast. I'll call in to work, and have them get a substitute to take my class. I'll tell them I have a family situation or something."

"Where shall we meet?" he asked.

So they made plans to meet at Janet's favorite coffee shop. By the time they finished the call, Janet sounded like she might explode from happiness at any moment.

When Anthony put his cell in his pocket, Becky hugged him tight. "I hate to sound cynical, but a vision?"

"I know. It sounds nuts and to think of how I used to make fun of people like Janet. But, it is what it is. I don't know how else to explain it."

"Do you want to talk about it?"

Anthony found that he did.

He sat at the table with Becky and told her everything he could remember about the vision. It was very vivid, and he could still hear the voice like an echo of thunder in his mind.

He told her about the instruction to find others like himself and the signs that were supposed to be revealed to him.

Becky leaned back and scrunched up her nose. "Are you sure about all of this? Are you sure you aren't *stressed* from the shooting?"

He smiled, wondering if it was God's sense of humor to awaken him in such a way, and then have him instantly butting up against the same sort of skepticism he'd always been so quick to dish out.

"I'm certain. There was no mistaking it. I know it was sort of a dream, but there was such a reality to it. As nuts as it sounds, God spoke to me. I understand how it must seem. But can you sort of just hang with me? Let me explore it. I've never been shaken like this."

"I know." She giggled. "I can see you're out of sorts."

"But in a good way?" He reached out and held her hands.

"Yes. In a very good way."

Ben pounded down the stairs dressed for the day but still looking tired.

"Good morning, slugger." Anthony reached to give his son a hug. "Be good for your mom this morning, okay?"

"Where are you going?" Ben asked.

"I'm having breakfast with Aunt Janet."

Ben's eyes crossed. "I thought you didn't like being alone with Aunt Janet."

Becky laughed and gave Anthony an *I told you so,* look.

"What gave you that idea?" Anthony asked.

"Well, you're always dodging her calls and

avoiding her."

*Out of the mouth of babes.* Hearing such a bold statement from his son was not funny at all, and it brought Anthony back around. "Yeah. That's true. But it's all changed now."

"Oh." Ben frowned.

"In fact," Anthony said, as he grabbed his Bible from the kitchen table and headed for the door. "A lot of things are going to start changing."

~*~

Anthony met Janet at the *Paducah Coffee Shop and Bakery* she had recommended.

Although he usually drank quite a bit of coffee, Anthony's nerves were far too edgy to enjoy a cup that morning. So instead, he opted for a calming cup of London Fog, a tea the barista recommended. He anxiously toyed with the string of the tea bag.

"My gosh." Janet blew on her coffee, giving him a nervous smile over the steam. "Just spill it already. You look like you're about to jump out of your skin."

He hesitated. "You're going to think I'm crazy."

"Maybe. Probably." She grinned. "That remains to be seen. What's on your mind?"

He took a deep breath and plunged in, trying his best to relay the events of the past few days, beginning with how he'd felt drawn to start reading the Bible when he came home from the hospital.

At that point Janet fairly beamed, making

Anthony wonder what she was going to look like when he got to the part about the dream.

He continued, telling her how scripture had seemed to come alive for the first time in his life. How he felt God Himself was actually speaking to him through His word.

And then he got to the vision. He felt his eyes tear up during several moments, particularly the part where he actively walked towards the cross in front of second base.

He kept sneaking glances at Janet as he recounted the dream and was surprised to see she was not gazing at him as if he'd lost his mind. In fact, she wept quietly through it all.

When he finished speaking, Anthony went back to picking at the string and the label from his tea bag. When he couldn't take the silence any more he asked, "Well?"

"What does Becky think?" Janet spoke at last.

"She's supportive. I think. I haven't gone into the full dream with her yet. She sort of believes me, I hope. But then again I sort of just gave her the overall view. I made it seem more like a vivid dream than"

"Rather than a vision?"

"I guess."

"Do you think that's what really happened though?" Janet asked. "A vision?"

"It was so real. And the people the man in the

first dream mentioned. I think I'm really supposed to find them."

"And after you find them? Then what?"

"That's it. God isn't exactly overwhelming me with a lot of information about how this is all supposed to go down."

Janet sat silently. What was she thinking?

She reached out and took his hand. "I believe every word of it. All throughout the Bible, God used dreams to speak to people."

She shut her eyes and then opened them again and focused on his face. "I'm not sure if you know this or not, but God rarely chose people who had their lives all perfectly wrapped up. All through Scripture, there's evidence that God used normal men and women."

"Like you?"

"As a matter of fact, He often used screwed up people. And some of them just downright didn't like Him very much."

"Why?" Anthony winced. "That doesn't make sense."

"It depends on who you ask. But I personally think it's to show His glory. He wants us to be able to see His transformative power. And if I might be so bold to say so, I believe I'm seeing that firsthand through you."

Anthony felt a tremble across his back. "I don't know what to do with this. What if I am no good at it? I just wanted to talk to you to make sure this sort of thing was, if it could be *real.*"

"I think it is."

"Thank you."

"One of the big gripes a lot of wanna-be believers have is why the Bible is filled with miracles to show God's might while the world around us seems to have none. But there *are* miracles every day. I think you're living one right now."

"It's starting to feel like it," he agreed.

Janet reached into her purse, pulled out her cell phone, and flicked through her contacts. "I'm going to text you the number to *New Beginnings*, the church I attend."

*Was he ready for this?*

"If you really fell led to try to act on this vision and need some spiritual discernment or direction, I'm sure Pastor Good would love to help you."

"This thing seems too personal. I felt weird enough calling you, much less a pastor I don't know."

"God will place people along your path to help you," she said. "I've seen it time and time again, but the media never really covers this kind of stuff, you know. No one walks alone when they walk with God."

"That sounds clichéd"

She shrugged. "Doesn't make it any less true."

He smiled. "Thanks for meeting with me. And

thanks for the support."

"Of course. I'm thrilled for you, and I'm glad to be involved. Any idea what your next step is?"

He shook his head. "No clue."

"That's okay. God will show you."

"Yeah." Anthony responded with a nervous chuckle. "That's exactly what I'm afraid of."

## CHAPTER 9

Anthony found it odd to be home alone.

The doctors wouldn't release him to go back to his office for at least four weeks after the surgery, and something about that seemed alien to a workaholic like him.

With Becky at her job at the dermatologist's office, and Ben at school, Anthony had the house to himself. So he sat down at the kitchen table and took out his cellphone, pulled up the number that Janet had texted him to New Beginnings and Pastor Good.

He considered calling right then and there. But the idea of telling someone else about the dream and what he was going through seemed like it would not only be exhausting, but a little embarrassing, too. Especially to a stranger.

In fact he felt a bit hazy with all the possibilities circling in his head. So Anthony did what the doctors had recommended. He went into the living room, stretched out on the couch, and rested.

It had been forever since he'd watched television in the morning, and he'd nearly forgotten the banality that was presented.

Talk shows, depressing newscasts, reruns of

terrible sitcoms. No wonder many Americans were turning into workaholics like him. But if this was the alternative, he didn't want anything to do with it.

Anthony settled on a news program that seemed to be middle-of-the road and without a blatant political agenda. He kept it on for nothing more than white noise and then went into the bedroom and retrieved his Bible.

He figured he should run a Google search or something to find out what sections of the Bible mentioned God speaking directly to people, or maybe even about the gift of revelation.

The more he mulled over it the more he knew that's what this whole thing felt like. He had been given instructions to do something particular, and he assumed there was a reason for it.

Yet there was still a small part of him that wondered if he might be going crazy. Things like this simply didn't happen to people like him. Did they?

As he walked back into the living room something on the news caught his attention.

It was more of the same—a sensational story aired at the top of the hour to rope in the sympathy-viewers. Anthony listened to the newscaster as he took his place back on the couch with his Bible.

"...in Clanston, Ohio where a drunk driver was the only survivor of a tragic three car accident that took the lives of a teenager and an elderly couple.

"Police say the inebriated driver, one Michael Reeves, was thrown from his car *after* it rolled over.

"Reeves was tossed directly into a tree, and his left shoulder was shattered. He had no other injuries, save a few scrapes and cuts, and he awaits what is likely to be a brutal trial when he is discharged from the hospital. In other news"

Not sure why the story had managed to get his attention, Anthony picked up his Bible and flipped to where he had last stopped in the book of Mark. There it was, he'd just started reading about the men who planned to lower someone through a roof

He felt a breeze and a sound like thunder boomed in Anthony's head. *"GO TO HIM."*

Anthony looked at the television, wondering if the voice had come from there. But no, it was just a reporter going over the highlights of last night's basketball games.

*"Go to him."*

He knew without a doubt *him* was referring to Michael Reeves. The name reverberated through his mind, leaving no doubt.

Before Anthony knew what hit him, he was standing and walking toward the laptop sitting on a small desk on the other side of the living room.

He needed to find out where Michael Reeves was staying and

And what? Well, it was terrifying, but he thought he knew.

## Awareness

He was supposed to find other people. People who had been through near-death ordeals like he had.

Michael Reeves had certainly had such an event. And how many more?

*But Ohio is several hours away. I have to call Becky and figure out who will get Ben from school and—*

*"Go to him."* The command came a third time.

"Yes, Lord."

With that he was committed. The burden of resistance off his shoulders, Anthony dashed to the bedroom to pack a bag.

On the way out to the car, he grabbed his cellphone and pushed the code for Becky. *How was he supposed to explain this situation?*

She answered, and taking no time to think he just blurted out what was on his heart.

"Becky, I know it seems crazy, but I am compelled to do this."

"What?"

"See, God instructed me to go find this guy named Reeves. He's a drunk driver from Ohio, who got into this terrible accident and killed three people in the process."

"Where did you say?" Becky's voice rose to a higher pitch.

"It was on the news today. It happened in Clanston, Ohio."

"And God told you, through the news channel, to go see someone in Ohio?"

"Yes. Michael Reeves."

"Anthony, honey, you don't even know this guy, and for that matter, you've never even been to Clanston, Ohio." With every sentence Becky's tone had changed from curious until now it was outright incredulous.

"I'm sure your doctors wouldn't approve of such a long drive. They haven't even released you to go back to work yet. Are you sure you're up to the trip?"

"But they also told me to let my body tell me how much I was up to doing." Anthony really had no choice because he had made a commitment to God.

"I know this is all very sudden and sounds insane, but Becky, please trust me. I've heard something, or someone speaking to me."

"If you go, when will you be home?" Her voice sounded defeated.

*Please Lord, let her understand.* "I really don't know, sweetheart."

*Silence.*

"I will call you when I get there and let you know what I find."

She sighed. "Well, that's it then. I don't seem to have an available husband any more than when you went to the bar every week-end."

A tiny speck of doubt surfaced. Chest aching from the depressing talk Anthony hung up the phone.

*It does sound crazy. If I were her, I wouldn't believe me either.*

~\*~

Anger built within Anthony as he drove toward interstate I-78.

"What's wrong with this guy? Drinking and driving? Did he think he was out on a sight-seeing tour?"

*Reeves killed an elderly couple and a teenager. And of course, he's barely injured. They should give him life and throw away the key. He's the worst of the worse. A dungeon would be too good for the likes of him.*

Anthony jammed his finger on the power button of his car radio. He kept it set on a Christian station these days.

"We're talking about a parable of Jesus from Matthew 18: verses 23 through 35."

Anthony turned up the volume to better hear the pastor.

"Here was a King who forgave one of his subjects. This king forgave the man a huge debt he could never pay back. Rather than throwing him in jail, this King *forgave the debt.* Then later this same former debtor threw another man, who owed him just a small debt, in jail without mercy."

The pastor's words caught Anthony like a strong punch in the stomach.

"When the King got word of the deed, he called the debtor whom he had forgiven and threw him in jail to be tormented **because he did not forgive as he was forgiven.**"

With a sinking heart, Anthony remembered his own episodes of drinking and driving in his old life. The life before Jesus.

Now that Anthony had been forgiven so graciously by God, how could he condemn Reeves, a man he didn't even know?

The lesson penetrated Anthony's mind and heart. With a flick of the turn signal he pulled off the road. Bowing his head he allowed tears of repentance to flow down his face.

"Oh, God, I could have been this man. How can I judge him when you have shown your mercy in forgiving me? I repent of this sin of self-righteousness. Please forgive me."

Peace and relief washed over him. "Thank you, God."

He'd never been a crybaby. Wasn't manly to show that kind of emotion. But lately he seemed to weep at the drop of a hat.

Anthony wiped his eyes then checked his GPS. According to the route information, he had a nine and a half hour drive ahead of him. No wonder Becky was shocked he had even considered the trip. He knew she just didn't get it.

It was almost noon, so he'd better grab something

to eat and fill the gas tank too. He'd only need to make one more stop before he reached Clanston.

~*~

With both his tank and his belly filled, Anthony resumed the journey.

A white shimmery cloud appeared in front of the Porsche and startled him. "What is this?"

*"I, the Lord, have called you. I will show you where to go and what to do,"* God spoke to his heart.

Anthony caught his breath. "Yes, God."

The cloud floated in front of his car, showing him where to turn, what lane of traffic to get into for the next exit, and when to merge.

When Anthony stopped for more fuel and food at 6:00 o'clock the cloud hovered over the car until he resumed traveling.

And when dusk fell the cloud became more slender and upright and picked up a rosy glow. *A cloud by day and a fiery pillar by night?* Anthony smiled at this latest showing of God's sense of humor.

At 10:00 that evening Anthony passed the Welcome to Clanston sign.

Of course, by then it was much too late to call Becky.

## CHAPTER 10

The next morning Anthony arrived at the hospital at 10:30 wondering what God had planned for him.

He entered the high rise parking lot, searching for a slot near the elevators. Several stories up he found what he was looking for on the Brown Level.

Visiting hours began at 11:00 a.m., and by the time he found the receptionist at the visitor's desk, Anthony was just in time. She told him Reeves's room number was 212.

Arriving on the second floor, Anthony followed the arrows to the room he needed.

But the door to Reeves's room was neither closed to indicate the patient was not to be disturbed, nor was it open to welcome visitors to walk right in. Instead, the door was slightly ajar, and Anthony hesitated.

"Help me, God," he whispered. Then he tapped on the door.

There was no answer from the room.

Anthony swallowed the lump in his throat and knocked louder.

"Yeah?" A gravelly voice came through the door. "What now? You got another pill to shove down my throat?"

# Awareness

*"There are demons in the room, but do not fear, I am with you,"* God spoke to Anthony's heart

Perspiration broke out on his face. He backed up against the wall outside the door. "What is going on?" he whispered. "A demon?"

*"I said do not fear. I am with you, and have given you the gift of discernment of spirits."*

Anthony swallowed the lump in his throat and moved toward the room again. This time he stuck his head inside.

A frowning middle-aged man with a scruffy brown beard, leaned on one arm, half-sitting up in the bed, and stared at him.

Then a very noticeable darkness began to fill the room and hovered over Reeves's bed.

*Whoa.*

A grotesque creature emerged from the darkness. Gnarled and twisted in its center, the demon had two heads. On the forehead of one was the word "ANGER", and on the other was the word "HATE." Both the demon's faces scowled at Anthony.

Without knowing why, Anthony stretched out his hand. He heard the scraping of metal, and a sword touched his hand. He wrapped his fingers around the scabbard.

The sword had a sleek silver blade engraved with *The Word of God.*

Anthony was covered in beautifully crafted, protective armor which fit him perfectly. He moved his arms. Amazingly, he felt completely comfortable.

Reeves continued to glare at Anthony but didn't indicate he saw anything out of the ordinary. "Yeah? You got something to say to me?" He eased back on the bed, clutching his shoulder, his eyes never leaving Anthony's face.

A chill came over Anthony's body. The demon above the bed of the patient, reminded Anthony he could not do this alone.

The cool silver metal of the sword in his hand also reminded him this wasn't an ordinary fight. And then peace covered him with a warmth like he'd never felt before.

"Are you Michael Reeves?"

"That depends on who's asking"

One of the demon faces scowled viciously at Anthony and the other wore a ghastly smile.

Anthony heard more metallic sounds, and the corner of his eyes picked up glimmers of light in the room.

"I am Anthony Markson."

"So? What's that to me? And why did you stick your head in here?" Reeves growled.

Now both of the demon's heads grinned evilly.

Anthony grasped the scabbard of the sword more firmly. "I just wanted to talk with you about your accident."

"Hey, you a detective or something? I've told the

police everything I could remember and that's not much." Reeves smiled faintly and let his eyes go shut. "I was pretty drunk." Then another scowl broke out across Reeves's face, "What's this about anyway?"

The demon twisted one of his heads from side to side as though mimicking Reeves's annoyance.

"It's all about God," Anthony replied without hesitation.

At the sound of the name of the Lord, the demon cringed, screeched, and hid both of his faces.

Anthony's heart pounded as though it wanted to come right out of his chest. He tightened his grip on the gleaming sword and stood firm.

The scowl on Michael Reeves's face deepened. "God? What's he got to do with anything?"

The demon shook at the second mention of that *name* and drew into a tight ball.

"Maybe nothing, maybe everything," Anthony answered.

Reeves's eyes widened. "You a preacher?"

"Nope. Far from it." Anthony chuckled.

"Well, what then?" Reeves made another attempt to sit up. He grimaced and grabbed his shoulder. "Get on with it. Tell me what you want or I'll call the nurse."

He reached for the call button, grabbed the bed sheet in a fist and tried to pull himself upright.

The creature unwound and surged to the forefront of the room, placing himself between

Reeves and Anthony. The demon's eyes glowed with fire. All four of them.

"I just want to talk. Tell me why you drink and let alcohol take control of you?"

"Control me? Control me? Nothing controls me, mister."

With Reeves's statement, the demon took a step forward and the coarse eerie sound of laughter filled the room.

Anthony thought Reeves was going to go for the call button again and then realized he had let go of the sheet.

Reeves lay back on his pillow as if exhausted. "I drink to forget."

Once again, the demon laughed. He twisted around and around and around, bobbing up and down in some form of dance.

"Forget what?" Anthony pressed. "What do you need to forget?"

Reeves narrowed his eyes. "Mister, why do you care? Who are you anyway?"

The demon stopped twirling, and both heads smirked at the question.

"I'm just a friend."

"I don't have any friends." Reeves's eyelids drooped.

The demon's grin became cadaverous, making a dark hole in both his faces.

"You have one now," Anthony said, as Reeves

drifted off to sleep. "I know for a fact that Jesus loves you."

The creature shuttered at Anthony's words and backed away. The darkness in the room lessened a bit.

"What a friend we have in Jesus." Anthony sang the words of an old hymn he remembered as a child.

When he finished, Anthony glanced around the room. Reeves still slept peacefully, the demon had disappeared, and the room was once again bathed in normal daylight.

Anthony backed into the hall and pulled the door shut. The sword that had been in Anthony's hand was gone but he still felt the essence of cool metal against his skin.

He leaned back against the wall. "Wow. That creature was an ugly thing. Thank you for the protection, God. The protection. Yes that was beautiful."

"Well done," God whispered to his heart, "You repelled *Mastema* the demon of hostility."

Anthony marveled at what had just happened. He pulled out his phone and dialed Becky, hoping to catch her on her lunch break.

"Well, did you find your Mr. Reeves?"

He smiled as her tired voice filtered into his ear.

"You sound tired. Rough day at work?"

"Just some office politics that I think we finally

settled. Hoping for a smoother afternoon. So how about you? Mission accomplished?"

"Yep, but I also found something else. Something really ugly in the process."

"Whatever does that mean?" she said. And then she yawned.

"It means I won't be home tonight. Seems I've been drafted into an Army."

"Okay, dear, see you tomorrow." Becky seemed distracted. Maybe she wasn't so confident about her afternoon.

As Anthony ended the call he heard "What?" Becky's voice rose.

But he had already closed the phone. Maybe he could find out what she was about to ask tomorrow.

With a twinge of guilt Anthony realized he wasn't so sure he'd be home tomorrow night either. Even though the demon had retreated for now, Anthony knew he would be back another day.

Later that night as he settled into his motel bed he hoped he could sleep but doubted the experience he'd had would allow it.

*I've held a sword in my hand, seen a demon, and I've recognized the reality of what really goes on behind the scenes. My life is never going to be the same again.*

## CHAPTER 11

Anthony knew the sword that protected him was *The Word of God.* All the answers to this new challenge in his life would be found there.

He spent most of the night searching through his Bible for scriptures to indicate what God would do next in his life. Somehow driven to the book of Ephesians, Anthony scoured the chapters until he found what he was seeking so desperately.

Ephesians 6:10 held the key to everything, including the very source of all the power he needed to do battle.

He needed much more than just the sword, and this verse taught the truth of putting on the whole armor of God. Anthony thanked God for revealing the secret.

Finally, Anthony drifted off to sleep but was awakened by the clanging of metal.

He'd heard the sound before, and he'd found himself holding a sword. But this time it was not the resonance of just one sword against another, but many.

When Anthony opened his eyes, the room was filled with soldiers. They stood at attention, all suited with a complete set of armor.

Anthony could not utter a word as he watched the warriors drop to one knee, bowing their allegiance to someone just above them.

A great light, that nearly blinded him, appeared between Anthony and the soldiers so that, for a moment, he could no longer see them.

"Arise, men, go where this one goes, for I have given him the gifts of inspiration. Follow as he leads. Do as I have commanded." It was the strong, yet strangely gentle voice of the Elite Commander.

The soldiers stood as one body, with swords drawn, as though ready for battle.

As the mighty army faded, the room became smaller and was, once again, a simple motel unit.

Anthony leaned back against his pillow. "Wow." An inner strength filled his being. Excitement surged through his body.

*I am seeing reality. God is revealing what is really happening.*

Glancing at his watch, he realized it was early morning. He hadn't had much sleep, but he could not waste a minute more.

He jumped up and carried his Bible with him to the breakfast area offered by the motel. After a quick meal he was soon headed for the hospital.

In no time he was slipping down the hall, approaching room 212.

The door was ajar this time as well, so he listened for anyone stirring about. He heard nothing and peeked into the room.

"Who are you?" a voice behind him, asked.

Without flinching, he turned and saw a short, matronly woman with her golden brown hair in some sort of up-do.

"Oh, sorry. I'm Anthony Markson."

"Why are you standing here peeping into my husband's room? Do you know him?" she asked in an accusing tone.

Darkness hovered behind her. Did she have a harassing demon too?

Anthony distinctly heard the sound of faraway laughter. Erie laughter.

*"It is time for battle,"* God spoke to him in a whisper.

"I really don't know him. I'm sorry. I was just hoping he was awake so I could talk to him for a few minutes."

"Well, why didn't you just knock?" She rolled her eyes to gaze up at him.

When he didn't answer, she reached around him and pushed on the door. It swung open to an empty room.

Just then a nurse walked around the corner wearing a breastplate engraved with the word *Righteousness*, over her uniform. At least an inch taller than his sister Janet, Her green eyes were full of compassion, and her smile was radiant. "Oh, Mrs. Reeves, are you looking for your husband? He's in x-ray."

The nurse glanced at Anthony. "Hello. My name is Abby Power. How can I help you?" And then he heard her soft voice call him, "Brother."

Anthony smiled. "I am a friend of Mr. Reeves. I just stopped by to speak with him."

"He'll be back in a few minutes. You can both wait in his room if you'd like."

Anthony was sure he glimpsed the scabbard of a sword at the very end of her uniform sleeve, as Abby turned and walked away.

"Thanks." Mrs. Reeves went into the room. The darkness followed her.

Maybe Mrs. Reeves could give Anthony some insight into her husband's situation but she definitely had need of deliverance herself. And, after all, he came here because God had called him to this task.

"I have given you a new name, Warrior," the Elite Commander had whispered. "Get ready for battle."

So Anthony knew he had to be prepared to fight soon. He could already feel the essence of smooth metal against his skin.

"Come on in." Mrs. Reeves broke the silence. "I want you to explain to me how you can be a friend of Michael's and yet not know my husband."

He joined her inside Michael's hospital room and took a seat in a straight-backed chair near the door.

With a weary smile on her face, she settled into a

recliner near the window.

As she leaned back in her chair, Anthony noticed the area underneath her. It became darker and darker until he realized it was an opening in the floor.

Out of the pit rose a huge, heavy chain. The end of the chain attached itself around Mrs. Reeves left leg.

Large drops of liquid splashed into the pit. Anthony looked up. The fluid was coming from Mrs. Reeves's light brown eyes. The pool of her tears kept widening until it almost reached Anthony's feet.

Sorrow. Deep sorrow bound her in chains.

"How did you meet my husband?" she asked.

"Actually. I just met him here last night."

"Here? But how? Didn't you know him before that?"

Anthony shook his head. "No. I just heard of him on TV."

Her eyes widened. "On TV. So what you're saying is you didn't even know him before he was on the news?"

"That's true. I didn't."

Seeing her incredulous expression, he added, "But I met him yesterday, and he seems to be an interesting man."

A frown formed on her forehead "Oh, you could say he's *interesting*, all right."

Suddenly the water around her feet gushed, swirled, and rose upward, until it soaked her legs.

The strange thing was she didn't seem to notice. Anthony stared at the vision of her in amazement.

"My husband is not a nice man. He has never been nice to me or anyone else. He's angry and depressed." She shuddered and looked at Anthony with wounded eyes. "It's all I can do to stay married to him. I hate him."

With those words, she put her hand over her mouth. "I can't believe I said that."

A demon jumped from the pit, hands on hips, and reared his head back cackling with laughter.

The hairs on Anthony's neck stood at attention.

The elf like creature perched on the edge of the pit, crossed his legs, and leaned forward. "You poor wretched soul," he spoke in mock sympathy. "How marvelous is your pain and sorrow."

Once again the gleaming silver sword was clasped into his right hand, real and cool to the touch.

A soft wide belt laminated with the word, TRUTH slid around his waist.

Then a helmet nestled on his head, and a shield appeared in his other hand.

The breastplate covering his heart and lungs was much like the one Abby had been wearing. His feet gleamed with warrior boots.

Anthony stood poised, but he didn't know what

he was supposed to do next. However he was clothed with the full armor of God, and he waited.

"I really don't hate Michael. I know it's wrong to hate anyone. But I am so tired of dealing with his ugliness toward me both physically and emotionally."

Then she added, "I'm sorry. I didn't mean to vent to you. I just haven't been able to talk to anyone since all this mess happened. With the accident and the deaths of those poor people." This time her tears were real.

As she continued to weep, the pool of water rose to her shoulders.

"I've suffered years of abuse from his hands. Years of physical, mental and emotional abuse. I am so miserable. I am desperate." Her teary voice trembled as the water swirled around her face.

Perdix, the demon of despair and sorrow swam upward with an expression of extreme vexation.

Mrs. Reeves began to cough and was obviously short of breath.

Anthony felt a protective surge of compassion. "You have a deep sorrow, and you've been dealing with it for a long time." His heart beat faster. Where had those words come from?

"I have given you the gift of wisdom," God spoke to his heart. "Use it judiciously."

Mrs. Reeves jumped to her feet. "How did you know that?" Her eyes became as saucers. "Who are you?"

Perdix frowned and yanked the chain attached to her leg.

She stumbled.

Anthony caught and steadied her. "Jesus will help you."

When Anthony grabbed the leg-chain, it fell apart as though it were made of paper.

The growling demon grew in size and attempted to grab her with his long curved fingers.

Anthony lifted his shield between himself and Perdix. He swung his sword and sliced off the demon's hand.

The waters receded.

The demon scurried frantically back into the pit with a curse.

The chains which had previously bound Mrs. Reeves were gone, and she eased back into her chair.

She glanced at Anthony with hope on her face. "Is that how you knew about me? Did Jesus speak to you?"

*Here is another one who knows Him.* Anthony nodded and smiled. "And that's how I know about your husband too. God has known about your sorrow for a long time. He's just been waiting for you to cry out to him about it."

"Please call me Deborah. I asked Jesus into my life as a little girl. But since then I've stumbled down a dark path. A very dark path. Can you do something to help me?"

"Sure. Let me pray for you." Anthony looked for her acknowledgment.

"It's like something ominous takes over, and I can hardly breathe. At times I'm really afraid I may die."

Anthony heard the marching steps of an army close by.

He bowed his head "Jesus, King of Heaven, I call on the authority that I have in you, to restore your daughter, Deborah. Strengthen her to resist the devil. I command Perdix, the demon of sorrow to be gone from her, never to return. By your blood and by your righteousness. Amen."

Anthony looked up as he finished the prayer.

Deborah had on the belt of Truth just like his. And a large surrounding army knelt on one knee.

The moment Deborah whispered, "Amen," the nurse, Abby, still wearing the breastplate of righteousness, wheeled Michael into the room.

Michael clutched the armrests of his wheelchair and wore his seemingly perpetual scowl. "Hey, what's going on in here?"

Deborah, Anthony, and the nurse simply smiled as Michael looked from one to the other.

"Well, done, my good and faithful servants. But don't put your armor away quite yet." The rushing wind of God's whispered voice floated into Anthony's ears.

Mastema, in the form of the Siamese twin demon

of Anger and Hate materialized from a dark cloud surrounding Michael.

Leaning over, the demon placed each head beside Michael's ears, and whispering with both his mouths, the demon enticed Michael's anger.

"They're mocking you."

"You're not gonna let them get away with that, are you?"

"You better show them who's in charge here."

Michael maneuvered his chair to the duffle bag at the edge of his bed. He made one swift motion with his good arm. "I've had enough of this nonsense."

And once again Anthony had a gun pointed right at him.

## CHAPTER 12

Abby extended her hand toward Michael. "Give it to me."

Michael's face blanched.

The room was silent until the nurse calmly spoke again. "Michael, in the name of Jesus, hand the weapon to me."

Anthony watched the demon Mastema fade into the floor, with much screaming and cursing.

Then, with a gentle movement, Michael, turned the gun around and placed the handle into the nurse's hand.

At that, Anthony and Deborah both breathed a sigh of relief.

Michael dropped his head in shame. "Please don't call the police." His voice trembled as if he might cry. "I was so angry and scared. I didn't mean to harm you. Not any of you." He glanced at his wife and then at Anthony. "I don't know what made me pull the gun."

"Brother Anthony, why don't you have a talk with these two while I find Lieutenant Collins?" Abby said before she swiveled to again face Michael.

"Don't worry. You'll have enough to deal with

when you get out of here without adding this business to the list. Having said that, I *will* have to turn this gun in, but I *don't* have to say you pointed it at anyone."

The gift of faith shone in Abby's smile. It was obvious she was truly confident in a power much stronger than her human ability.

He could use someone like her on his side in these battles.

As the nurse left the room, Anthony turned to Michael. "Suppose you tell me about your anger and what you think causes it."

Anthony spent the rest of the morning talking to Michael and Deborah.

God revealed much about what was going on with them to Anthony's heart by giving him the gift of knowledge.

By the time another nurse came in to give Michael his medicine, Anthony knew a lot more about the middle aged couple. Like others before him, Michael had let alcohol take control of his life.

The demon of anger and hate was the cause of his drinking as well as the result. So it was a vicious cycle.

The alcohol fueled what was already working in Michael's life to bring him down even farther.

And what was his real undoing was that Michael tried overcoming it all with his own human power.

He admitted to being abusive to Deborah and

with tears, he reached for her hand and apologized to her.

By that time Deborah was weeping as well. But they seemed to be good tears this time.

Anthony looked at them. "I don't understand everything yet but from what I've experienced the last few weeks, no one can fight and win this type of battle within his or her own power."

"Maybe." Michael shook his head. "But it seems like if I was any kind of man, I could."

"There you go, beating up on yourself. You need to stop that my friend. God wants a personal relationship with each of us. I know this because He's spoken to me audibly as well as whispered in my heart."

"That's heavy." Michael shook his head in wonder. "It seems unreal to be able to say you know God personally."

"I know the name of Jesus gets rid of the demons that cause us to be people that we don't really want to be. I know armor is available, and a powerful shield of protection, which covers us when we're willing to let God fight our battles for us."

"Is that what just happened? Did God use you and Abby to fight my battle?"

"Well it sure wasn't any of my own doing. God gives me visions showing what's going to happen and what the reality of the situation is."

"Heavy."

"I'm going to study a lot more about this when I get home." Anthony held up his Bible. "And I know where to find the answers."

Michael reached for Deborah's hand. "My wife will help me study." He glanced at her, "Won't you?"

Deborah nodded.

"Right now I know I need Jesus, and the only way to have Him, is to call on Him. Reality is not what can be seen with our eyes," Anthony said.

"I am so thankful for what Jesus did for me today." Deborah glanced at her husband. "For Michael and me both."

"After I dig deeper into the truth written here in the Bible, I'll come back to show you what I've learned, if you are willing to hear it."

They both nodded.

"I have a feeling you just saved our marriage, and possibly our lives." Deborah wiped a tear from her face.

Anthony shook his head. "No. Only the name of Jesus can do that. In fact we might all be part of an army God is raising up."

On the way back to the motel Anthony couldn't get Abby's faith out of his mind. How could anyone have known Michael wouldn't fire the gun? Then Anthony recalled the glimmer of armor. She was a warrior, or she was certainly on her way to becoming one.

Anthony basked in the knowledge that God had

spoken to him over the past couple of days.

He was sent here to meet Michael. Surely God had a work for him to do as well. And what about Deborah? Did she have a special gift too? Was she to be a part of God's army?

Anthony had seen her belt of Truth. He grinned. At the very least she would be a huge support for Michael, just as Becky would support him, once she heard the powerful manifestations of God.

Now that the present crisis seemed to be past, it was time to call home. Anthony punched Becky's number on his cell phone. She answered almost immediately.

"Hi, Honey. I was just calling to let you know I'll be heading home soon."

"Well, it's a good thing," she answered breathlessly. "You'd better hurry."

"Becky, what's wrong."

"I'm on my way to the hospital with Ben. It's his asthma."

"Hey, I just reached my motel. I'll check out and head on," Anthony said. "It took me ten hours to get here, but I'll try to shave a bit off of that time on my way home. Pray I don't get into a wreck or stopped for speeding. Tell Ben I love him, and that he'll be okay."

"No, Anthony, I won't tell him that, because he is not okay." Becky had steel in her voice. "I'm looking in the rear-view mirror now. Ben's thrashing from side to side because he can't breathe. You should be here where you belong."

Anthony heard the click as she ended the call. Would he lose his family because of this mission? "God, don't let anything happen to Ben. Help me get home quickly and safely."

Perspiration formed on his forehead. Where was God now? For him and his family? For Ben?

"Jesus, help me."

It took two-thirds the time for Anthony to get to the hospital in his hometown as it had taken to get to where Michael had been. Anthony couldn't believe a patrolman hadn't pulled him over.

It was only 7:00 o'clock in the evening when he jumped out of the car. God had been with him after all.

He pushed the hospital's double doors open and rushed inside to the Emergency Department.

A nurse looked up with an expression of alarm as he burst in.

"I've just arrived from Ohio. My six-year-old son is in this hospital somewhere. Can you help me find him?"

"I'll do my best. What is your youngster's name?"

"It's Ben. Ben Markson."

"They're getting a room ready for him upstairs, but meanwhile your family is still in cubicle one." She stood up. "Let me show you where they are."

He found the cubicle crowded as Ben was

undergoing a respiratory treatment. Janet stepped out to make room for Anthony.

Ben was pale and gasping for air.

"How long has he been like this? You've been here seven hours, right?"

Becky glared at him. "Some help you are. I was trying to keep him calm."

Anthony's heart raced as he stood beside his son. This was bad. The worst he had ever seen Ben look. "Oh, God," he prayed. "Don't let anything happen to our son."

Anthony felt someone's hand on his shoulder. "Ben will be okay," a voice penetrated his mind.

"Thank you, God," he whispered.

"He's not out of the woods yet, Anthony." His wife's voice was strident.

"He will be."

Becky looked skeptical, but it was just a few moments before Ben began to breathe easier.

He opened his eyes. "Dad, you're home."

'Yep. Now you just lie quietly, and breathe the medicine in. You will be okay in just a bit, and we'll see if we can find you some ice cream."

"Yeah." Ben said with a little difficulty.

"Don't try to talk just yet, Ben." Becky touched her son's shoulder. "Dad and I are going to step across the hall and discuss some things. Aunt Janet will come back in with you. So just keep breathing deeply. Okay?"

Becky gave Anthony a pointed look and tilted her head toward the space outside the cubicle.

"When did this latest episode start?" Anthony asked before she could start with any questions of her own.

"I heard Ben choking as I woke up this morning, and I rushed upstairs to check on him. He scared me so badly." She shook her head. "You'd think that as many times as I've been through this with him, I would be used to it."

"You mean it's been this bad before?"

"It's never lasted this long," Becky admitted.

Ben improved steadily with the latest respiratory treatment, and it wasn't long before he was finished and begging for ice cream."

An orderly arrived at the cubicle with a hospital bed. "We're ready to transfer you to pediatrics, young man."

Anthony lifted Ben from the cot in cubicle one and placed him on the hospital bed.

"I'll order some ice-cream to be delivered to his room," the ER nurse said.

Ben grinned from ear to ear as the orderly wheeled him away.

"You can go to the pediatrics waiting room until he gets settled," the nurse continued. "Shouldn't be too long. The room number is 359, and they will leave the door open when you're free to enter."

"Thank you." Becky tossed her long black hair

and walked out of the Emergency Department oblivious to whether Anthony or Janet followed.

"Hey," Janet called. "Wait up."

When she reached her sister-in-law, Janet looped her arm through Becky's elbow as if to keep her from running off.

Then Janet turned her attention to Anthony.

"So what do you have to tell us about the past four days?"

"Oh, I have a lot to share with both of you."

When he told about his first meeting with Michael and the demon that had floated above his head, Becky began to tremble.

She stopped walking. "Anthony, how scary. I had no idea you would be in so much danger."

"That's just it, Becky, I wasn't in any danger."

She gave him a *get real* look. "No danger? A demon? Right. You saw it. The creature was shrieking at you, and you weren't in danger. Right."

Janet nudged him with one elbow. "Anthony, what in the world"

"Wait. Just wait." He held up both hands. "Before I even went into Michaels's hospital room, God told me what I would encounter."

"God told you?" Becky snorted. "Did you actually hear a voice?"

Anthony winced at her scorn. "I did that time, but other times He spoke to my heart."

When Anthony told them about the vision of the

army kneeling in the motel room, Becky rolled her eyes.

"Becky, it's true. I saw those soldiers with their silver armor, holding swords, and kneeling. I saw a bright light all around and heard the one named the *Elite Commander* giving orders for them to protect me."

Becky unlinked her arm from Janet and rushed down the hall. Anthony let her go. She probably needed some space to be able to absorb his news, before they all met in Ben's room.

"Anthony, are you telling me God has guided you in all of this?" Janet asked.

"Oh, yes. I know He did. When I called on Jesus' name, the demon curled up, and when I kept mentioning God and Jesus and singing hymns, the demon disappeared."

"Wow. What a story."

"Oh, there's much more," Anthony answered. "I haven't even told you about Deborah's demon, or that I chopped its hand off, or the nurse who was able to take a gun away from Michael."

Becky had walked back to them "A gun?" She stepped back in horror. "Another gun? When will this end?"

"Well, it's not over yet because I promised to study up a bit and then go back."

"Go back?" The women said in unison.

Becky shook her head. "You can't go back."

# Awareness

"I have to, sweetheart. God is calling me into His army, and this is spiritual warfare. How else will people know what is really going on in their world? Reality is not always what we can see."

Becky twisted her hands together. "What will happen when you go back?"

"I don't know, Becky, but it will be exciting. I've got a lot of studying to do in God's word because my life has changed forever."

"Ya' think?" Janet replied, "Well, that makes two of us, I guess."

"Are you getting involved in this too?" Becky's voice rose in alarm as she looked at her sister-in-law with wide eyes.

"Can you think of anything more worthwhile in these days?" Suddenly, Janet's face began to shine.

And Anthony glimpsed a sword glimmering in the sun through the window at the end of the hall.

# CHAPTER 13

The three adults gathered around Ben's bed. His healthy coloring was back, and he grinned between bites of ice cream.

Anthony glanced out the window. "You have a great view here, buddy. I expect we'll have to drag you back to your own room tomorrow."

Ben laughed and suddenly made the awful wheezing sound his family had learned to fear. Then he began to cough.

"Ben!" Becky screamed.

He collapsed on the bed, and large whelps appeared on his face and arms. When he wasn't coughing, he gasped for breath.

Becky turned to Anthony, "Get his EpiPen out of my bag."

Anthony jerked around, grabbed Becky's bag, and frantically searched for the pen. His heart pounded with overwhelming fear before his fingers touched it. He snatched it up and took it to her.

Holding Ben in her lap, Becky opened the pen and stuck it into Ben's thigh.

Anthony felt the silver sword in his hand. He began to feel the fear drain from him, but it had nothing to do with Ben receiving his medicine through the EpiPen.

"Fight like a Warrior," God spoke to his heart. "Be sober, be vigilant; because your adversary the devil, as a roaring lion, walketh about, seeking whom he may devour" (1Peter 5:8).

Anthony glanced down. The armor of the Lord covered him, and there was strength in his arms and legs that he had never felt before.

Then he glanced at Ben, and his heart broke. A dark and evil spirit surrounded him.

"Oh, God, not Ben." Anthony pleaded aloud. "You said he would be alright."

"Fear not," God spoke with a great thunder in His voice. "Samael will not win. The battle is ours."

Ben continued to struggle for breath, and Becky's eyes widened in terror. "The medicine isn't working. I pushed the call button for help."

A power, far greater than the love of a mother or father, was wrapped around Ben's chest, tightening with every tick of the clock.

Ben's eyes rolled back until only the whites showed.

With no time to wait for a doctor or nurse, Anthony opened his mouth. "Let him go," he thundered.

The dark, ugly presence shot up, and the head of a twisted snake rose from Ben's chest. With green eyes flashing, his face hovered just a few inches from Anthony's. "By whose authority?" he hissed and showed long fangs, "*I* serve Apollyon. Who are *you* to command me to do anything?"

Anthony extended his sword with boldness and a determination like steel. "I serve Jesus Christ of Nazareth, and in His name I command you to let this child go."

At the name of Jesus, the demon-snake blinked. With one slice of the sword Anthony knocked off the snake's head, and it bounced across the room.

The snake body uncoiled from around Ben, and slithered over to the corner of the room, where both the body and head of the snake faded to nothingness.

"How can I help you?" The booming voice from the intercom startled the adults.

"My son is having another asthma attack," Becky screamed.

Ten minutes later, Ben had an oxygen mask on his face, an IV dripping into his arm, and a respiratory therapist worked with him once again.

Ben had a little more color in his face but was still in serious condition.

Becky wept inconsolably, and Anthony wrapped his arms around her.

"It's okay, he's going to be alright," he whispered to the top of her head.

"How do you know that?" She looked up at her husband and then lowered her face and covered it with her hands. "I'm scared, Anthony."

# Awareness

"Don't be afraid. God has spoken to my heart. He assured me Ben will be alright."

"Does this have anything to do with the other stories you told us?"

"Yes, Janet, it does."

"Well, that settles it. You are not going back. You cannot put yourself or the rest of us in danger. I won't have it." Becky's voice trembled, and then she cried uncontrollably.

"Becky, sweetheart. Listen to me. It's okay. I know you are exhausted. I'm staying here with Ben tonight. Nothing else is going to happen to him. He is going to be fine, trust me. No. Trust God."

"I'm not sure I can trust anyone. Guns. Demons. More guns. More demons. Why us? Why you? What next?" With eyes flashing anger, Becky turned to go.

Anthony caught her arm. "Can we talk about this later? Let's just concentrate on what the doctor can tell us right now. Okay?"

Becky wiped her eyes and nodded. She slid into one of the chairs near Ben's bed.

Janet sat on the floor beside Becky.

Glancing at Ben, Anthony saw he was breathing evenly, and his normal color had returned to his face.

He faced the doctor. "Doc, can you tell us anything?"

"I can tell you I have never seen a patient in such bad shape recover as quickly as this one."

"Well, I'm glad you were on duty tonight," Anthony said. "You must have been at the top of your class in medical school."

"This had nothing to do with me, my friend. Someone upstairs is looking out for your son."

Anthony flicked a glance at Becky then prayed aloud, "Lord, God, thank you."

"We will monitor his breathing and vitals tonight and see how he is in the morning."

As the doctor walked away, Janet eased up and moved to Anthony's side. "It was another demon attack, wasn't it?"

"Yes." Then looking into his sister's face, he asked, "How did you know?"

"God's been saying a few things to me too."

Anthony grinned. "Really?"

"Yep. The battle is the Lord's," Janet quoted one of the very verses God had spoken to Anthony.

"Wow. That is so neat. I am so excited." He squeezed his sister's arm.

"Your wife isn't."

The siblings turned, and Becky frowned at both of them.

Anthony cleared his throat. "Honey, they want to monitor him overnight."

"There is nothing wrong with my hearing." Becky stood and moved toward them. "And I'm not pleased with what I've heard."

"Becky, I promise"

"Don't make promises you can't keep, Anthony." Becky turned and went to her son's bedside.

Ben opened his eyes. "Mama, did you see the snake?"

Becky's eyes widened, and her mouth dropped open.

"Out of the mouth of babes." Janet looked at Anthony, and they shared a bittersweet smile.

"That was the biggest, ugliest one I ever saw. It was bigger than Spiderman. And it almost got me." Ben's voice rose with excitement. "But Dad saved me. Did you see his long sword? Did you see him whack the ole' snake?"

"Ben, don't get yourself all worked up," Becky warned. "I want you to rest now."

"But, Mama" he whimpered.

"Ben, you heard me. Calm down. I'll go get you something to drink."

Becky glanced at the adults in the room. "I'll get him a Sierra Mist, and I'll talk to the two of you tomorrow." She continued across the room and out into the hall.

Janet glanced at Anthony "Becky will be okay. She just needs to get used to it."

"You think she can?"

"We'll pray about it," Janet said. "Look what prayers have done for you."

"Yes, you're right. We will pray for her."

Becky brought Ben his Sierra mist and

offhandedly told Anthony and Janet goodbye.

"Walk her to the car," Janet urged. "We can talk when you get back."

Anthony rushed out of the room and slid up beside Becky in the hall. "I'm sorry you had to go through such a stressful and tiring day."

"You *say* you're sorry, but you're not. Not really."

Anthony should have learned a long time ago to let a statement like that go. But either he was a glutton for punishment or he was a slow learner.

Besides, she'd wounded him. "How can you say that?"

"Ben suffered off and on all day long. All. Day. Long. Then *you finally* get here and pray and within minutes he's better, at least, until that last stinking attack. What if the so called demon episode had come earlier? Before you got here? What then? Why can't you get it through your head that your family needs you here?"

"And I'll be here for at least a week because I have to do some heavy duty scripture research to prepare for what's ahead."

"Whatever." Becky got into her car and slammed the car door.

Ben was asleep when Anthony returned to the hospital room.

"What did you see tonight?" Anthony asked Janet as she pulled her chair up beside his.

"I'm pretty sure I saw most of it." Janet waved her

hands as she spoke. "Becky ran over to Ben, and then when the EpiPen didn't work, I witnessed that thing, the snake, winding like a tourniquet around Ben's chest. No wonder he was having trouble breathing."

"Then the snake tormented you about who was in charge. I heard what you said about Jesus Christ being who you served. You said that aloud, didn't you? I'm sure Becky heard it."

Anthony nodded, amazed and thrilled by the fact his sister understood and had witnessed so much of the battle.

"I also saw your armor and your sword. Boy, did you ever look like a warrior. And all around you an army stood at attention, as though they were waiting for a signal to draw their swords."

Anthony looked at Janet in astonishment. "You mean you saw the army? You saw something I didn't see."

"I did? Oh, this is priceless. You really couldn't see them?"

"I've seen them before but not this time." He reached out and squeezed her arm. "I guess I was so concentrated on Ben and what the snake was doing to him, I didn't see anything else. But Janet, this means you've been given the gift of discernment of spirits."

Janet's eyes widened as she absorbed her brother's words. "Well, if you didn't see them, I guess you didn't hear the talking either?"

"I didn't hear a thing. What did they say?"

"When you picked Ben up, they said, 'Well done, Warrior.' And also, Warrior was written on the right upper arm of your armor."

Anthony looked at her and felt his heart try to jump out of his chest. "Wow." Chills ran down his spine. *I am not worthy, but God has made me their leader, and He has given me a new name.*

"Janet?"

"Yes?"

"Are you in this with me?"

"Absolutely. I'm on your team."

As soon as Janet left the hospital room. Anthony pulled out his Bible and began a crash course in spiritual warfare.

Anthony prayed for increased knowledge of the Holy Spirit.

When he finally slept that night, it was with his chair pulled up to the side of Ben's bed and his head on one of Ben's extra pillows.

Anthony knew there would be another challenge when he got Ben home in the morning and faced Becky.

## CHAPTER 14

It was noon before they managed to leave the hospital the next day.

"Ben, in about a week I have to go back to Ohio to see the people I have been helping."

"Do you have to?" Ben frowned. "I don't want you to leave."

"I know but it's my job to help these people."

"But, Dad. You already have a job. You work here, in a big office."

The very thought of the office politics made Anthony wince. "I do. That is, I did until I was hurt. But God has called me to a different kind of job, and He wants me to be in Ohio now."

"God? You mean the God in heaven is your boss now?" Ben asked with widened eyes.

Anthony nodded.

"Neat." What's He sayin'? What kind of work does He give you?"

"Lots of things, Ben." Anthony laughed at Ben's big eyed expression.

"Is it about the snake that almost got me?"

"Well, not exactly about the snake but its other things that are kinda like it. See, He wants me to help other people like I helped you."

"Gee, that's neat. Can I come with you? I want to help too."

"Not now, son. Maybe when you are older. But this time, can you help Mom understand why I have to go?"

"I'll try, Dad. You know that's not going to be easy."

"I know." He tousled Ben's hair. "You can pray for me."

"Pray? Pray for you, Dad?" Ben's voice was filled with wonder.

"Yes. I'm counting on you."

Ben puffed out his chest. "I got your back, Dad."

It was all Anthony could do to hold in the chuckle that wanted to explode from his throat. "Thanks, son."

"You need to teach me how to be a warrior like you. Then I can watch out for Mom while you're gone."

Anthony's heart swelled. Ben had to grow up much too fast, but he seemed to be up to the task. Thanks to God, his Abba Father.

"God will teach you, if and when He thinks you are ready. But I doubt your mom will ever be ready for that."

When they pulled into the drive, Becky was outside waiting.

Anthony turned to his son. "Ben, promise me to keep going to church with Aunt Janet."

"I will. Aunt Janet and I will both be praying for you, Dad."

Becky opened the passenger door. "Hey, you," she said to Ben. "How are you feeling?"

"Better, Mom." Ben sprinted through the front door and ran towards his room.

He stopped at the top of the stairs. "Dad, don't leave again before I can hug you goodbye."

"I won't, son."

Anthony tried to meet Becky's eyes, but she turned away and headed for the kitchen.

He followed her. "Becky, we need to talk. Please. Come sit with me on the couch."

She settled herself onto a chair at the table. "Here is just fine."

Anthony tried not to grimace as he sat across from her. "Becky—"

"I want to say something first." She didn't wait for him to answer. "Anthony, I want you to stay home the remainder of this week and rest. Then you need to go back to work. To your firm. The place that supports us. I am so sick of this spooky stuff. I want my family back. I want things to go back to normal."

"Sweetheart, this is my normal now, and I would like to talk to you about it."

"Well it's not *my* normal." Becky stood up. "I don't want to hear about demons, guns or any of that."

"I have to go back to Ohio in the next week,

Becky. Let's not fight before I go."

She looked at him, "I just want my husband back."

"I'm still your husband, but I don't want to be the way I was before. You didn't want me to stay that way, remember? Now God has given me a purpose and a calling, and I'm committed to Him."

"Fine," she snapped. "Why wait? Go and do what you have to do but don't expect me to like it. I have your son to support." Her words were drenched with sarcasm.

She turned and left the room.

He'd hoped for a good talk with his wife and a good night's rest in his own bed, but it was not to be. Instead, Becky dropped sheets on the couch, and that's where Anthony spent the next few nights.

The house was peaceful during the day while Becky was at work. Anthony did most of his scripture reading then.

Ben was a trouper and wanted Anthony to read the Bible each evening. Becky sat through the chapter reading, which gave a semblance of togetherness, but when Anthony began to explain what he was learning, she left the room.

Finally, on Friday morning Anthony felt an urging in his spirit. It was time to head back to Ohio. He went into their bedroom to pack, and then took the stairs to say goodbye to Ben before he left for school.

# Awareness

Anthony found himself driving back to Ohio with a heavy heart. But he didn't get far down the road before He heard from God.

"My peace, I give unto you; not as the world giveth, give I unto you. Let not your heart be troubled, neither let it be afraid," Jesus voice spoke audibly to Anthony as though He was sitting next to him in the car.

It was the most gentle and caring voice. Peace and joy flowed over Anthony from his head to his feet and he was strengthened. He glanced over to see if he could literally see God sitting beside him.

And he made record time getting back to Ohio. It was as though he had simply blinked, and he had arrived at his destination. But in reality, when he checked his watch it was ten hours since he'd left New York.

He checked in at same motel, he'd stayed before.

This time as he studied the scriptures before falling asleep God spoke to his heart and told him not to go to the hospital because Michael had already been released.

## CHAPTER 15

Anthony was getting used to God's nudges, so it was no surprise when he pulled into a driveway and saw Deborah in the yard trimming a hedge. She looked up as he stopped close to where she was working.

"Get out and come in, Anthony. We wondered when you might come back."

"Well, I didn't know either, but here I am."

Deborah laughed and motioned for him to join her. "There's been a big change in Michael since he got home from the hospital. We've been studying our Bible together every day."

Anthony grinned. "That's great."

"Let's go inside," Deborah said, as she pushed open the front screen door. "He's anxious to talk to you."

Anthony looked inside, and sure enough, there sat Michael on the couch, reading his Bible.

He looked up and motioned Anthony over.

Deborah left the men in the living room and went into the kitchen.

"It's great to see you again, Michael," Anthony said holding out his hand. "How's the shoulder?"

"Still hurts some but I'm good." Michael had yet

to look Anthony in the eye. "About what happened in the hospital, I was rude to you, and the gun—"

"Listen, Michael, there is much you don't know about my life. Even my coming to see you the first time was strange, but something has drawn our lives together. Actually, I think it's someone.

Michael nodded.

"I saw what you've been fighting, and I'm here to help in a battle you know nothing about. I only know that I am to be your friend and help you out in all of this."

Michael looked puzzled and then took a deep breath. "I feel like I've been losing this battle all of my life. The alcohol, the hate and anger—"

Abruptly Michael's voice stopped, and a distinct roar came from the other side of the room.

The door of the cabinet in the corner swung open, and Ipos, in the shape of a panther with sharp, snow-white teeth stepped out.

His head swayed from side to side, and his emerald eyes blinked. "Michael, do you really think anyone can keep us from our old friends?" The growling question pierced the air.

Michael whispered to Anthony, "That cabinet is my home bar, where I kept my liquor."

Anthony extended his arm, and the sleek silver blade appeared, followed by the helmet, then his whole set of armor.

The demon panther slowly stepped backwards

but only a few inches. With teeth gleaming, he roared. His tongue, as a long jagged blade, came out of his mouth.

"I've been living with you for a long time, and I don't give up easily. Just have a sip of what you say you've given up. One taste won't hurt," he challenged Michael with a sneer. His eyes filled with mockery. "Come on, you know you want to." He lifted up one black paw that held a beer stein. "Let's have fun like we used to."

Michael had stood to his feet when the panther first appeared. Now he stumbled back a few feet and was eerily quiet, as if he was actually considering the challenge.

Would Michael allow all of this to destroy him?

"Holy Spirit, Help me." Anthony silently implored his Elite Commander.

"Stand firm, I am with you and will never leave you," answered the Spirit.

Then Anthony turned and faced the creature. A tremendous strength filled him.

"It's time to battle for Michael's life," the Spirit whispered.

Anthony did not hesitate. "Leave him alone," he commanded the dark and very powerful creature.

"And just who are you?" the demon panther asked Anthony with a savage roar.

Out the corner of his eye, Anthony noticed the army encamped about him. Two of the soldiers stood beside him, ready to do battle.

Anthony became bolder, swinging his saber as he stepped toward the demon.

The panther lunged and swiped his claw down Anthony's arm which held the sword.

Anthony yelped, and the sword fell to the floor, plunking on the carpet as his arm dripped blood.

The panther began prowling around and around Anthony, and he knew the creature had targeted him for a killing pounce.

Michael remained speechless and apparently couldn't move.

Suddenly the panther turned away from Anthony and pounced on Michael, throwing him on his back.

Michael used his arms defensively trying to protect his face. But the animal's teeth tore into his neck. Blood poured from his wound, and he tried to crawl away.

"Stop. Get off of him in the name of Jesus." Anthony shouted at the beast. He picked up his sword and brought it down on the panther's neck.

The severed head rolled, screaming and cursing, across the floor toward the cabinet and slammed into it. Flames shot into the air. Then the whole ugly scene disappeared.

Deborah ran out of the kitchen and over to Michael who by now seemed lifeless. She grabbed his wrist. "I feel a faint pulse."

"Call 9-1-1, and get an ambulance on the way."

Anthony said. Then he began rescue breathing.

Deborah found Michael's cell phone and punched the numbers frantically.

Seven minutes later the paramedics were there. After emergency treatment they loaded him on a stretcher and into the ambulance.

Once at the hospital, it didn't take long for Anthony's arm to be cleaned, stitched and bandaged. Then he sat in the waiting area with Deborah, wondering when the doctor would tell them anything about Michael.

"What happened?" Deborah asked. "I felt an evil presence and saw blood running down your arm. Then blood all over the floor as well. And poor Michael—"

"God was protecting you, Deborah."

~*~

Michael floated in a dark tube. Although his eyes were open, all he could see was darkness.

A far away voice called his name. The voice didn't sound like his friend Anthony.

"Michael, are you ready to be released?" the unfamiliar voice asked. "Are you tired of fighting against me?"

Michael strained to see who was speaking with no results.

Suddenly a bright light streamed through a hole in the tube. Michael floated closer and closer toward the light and finally reached its source.

# Awareness

At least with the light Michael could see he had been hurt. And there seemed to be a place of peace and rest on the other side of the tube.

He felt deep pain as he placed both hands on the opening and tried to heave himself through it to reach the peaceful place beyond. But something caught his feet.

He tried to kick it away. "Let go," he yelled.

Every time he got a little leverage to propel himself through the opening, something grabbed his feet and jerked him back.

"Help me, I want to get through," he cried. "I don't want to stay in this darkness. Somebody, help me."

Suddenly a hand grabbed him. His feet were free. He was propelled upward and out of the tube, leaving the darkness behind.

Energy and peace flowed through his body. Michael felt more alive now than he ever had before. He laughed and closed his eyes, enjoying the feeling.

"Michael, you are not ready for this trip's itinerary. There is much work to do if you make the cut."

Michael opened his eyes and found himself in the Emergency Department of the hospital. A unit of blood dripped into his left arm, and another IV infused something else.

A bandage felt tight against his neck, and a blood

pressure cuff squeezed his arm painfully.

"Doctor, he's coming around," a female voice said.

Then a bright light flashed in Michael's eyes. He blinked.

"Hold still," the doctor said, as he held Michael's eye open. "You seem okay, but I have to examine your reflexes."

After he examined Michael's eyes he listened to his chest and breathing.

"Where's Deborah?" Michael asked.

The doctor nodded, and a nurse slipped from the room.

In minutes Deborah leaned over and planted a kiss on his cheek.

"Doctor?" she asked in a trembling voice.

"He's okay, Mrs. Reeves. At least he will be if he keeps the wound bandaged tight until I see him in three days."

"Does this mean you're sending him home already?"

"Rest, plenty of liquids, food when he feels up to it. Then in five days we can see if it's healing okay and determine a time to take the stitches out."

"Whatever you say, Doctor. He will definitely have to rest and drink liquids on my watch."

"If you see blood seeping through the bandage, get him right back over here. You have to understand, your husband came close to having his carotid lacerated. He's a lucky guy."

# Awareness

"Blessed, doctor. Blessed," Deborah replied, touching Michael's hair.

"I'll send the nurse in with some medication for the pain and to prevent infection."

"Thank you, Doctor."

"Probably in another hour the IVs will be done, and the nurse can remove the lines. After all that, your husband can go."

Then the doctor spoke to Michael directly, "I don't know what kind of animal tried to have you for lunch, but don't go hunting for him again."

He turned to Anthony who had walked up, "Good job with the rescue breathing. Your friend would not have made it without that."

Anthony nodded.

"Oh," the doctor added, "take care of the arm."

"Yes, sir." Anthony promised.

Michael smiled at them, but soon his thoughts turned to the danger he had been in. His wife and friend did not know about his close brush with eternity.

Deborah and Anthony left the room. The ER nurse dimmed the lights so Michael could rest. Still, the whole scene kept going through his mind.

He could still hear his rescuer's voice and feel his hand lifting him through the opening. Suddenly the voice spoke again—this time to Michael's heart.

"Michael, you have a decision to make."

"Who are you?"

"I am the Elite Commander who rescues men from hell, and in return, gives them life. I am the Name whereby a man must be saved."

"Lord, I've made a mess of my life"

"Yes, you have, and I can help you win that battle. Do you want to be a winner?"

"Yes, Lord, I do. But I don't know how" Tears flowed down Michael's face.

"Do you believe I gave my life to give you eternal life?" the voice asked. "Do you believe I am the only one with that kind of power?"

"Yes, Lord, I do. Will you give me that life?"

"I will," the Elite Commander answered.

"Thank you, Lord, thank you," Michael whispered.

~*~

It was a quiet ride home for the three of them, but Anthony knew it would not stay quiet for very long.

He was thinking about the gift he'd been given—not only being a part of the Kingdom, but the ability to know what the Holy Spirit was doing in the Kingdom. He also knew with each gift came larger responsibility. *I wonder what other gifts I have been given.*

Deborah sat in the driver's seat and glanced at their guest in the rearview mirror. "Anthony, why don't you stay with us for a few days?" she asked. "We have a guest suite where you will probably be comfortable, and you may need to get your arm checked again."

"Yeah, friend, please do," Michael said.

"I'll have to check out of my motel, but you've twisted my arm. Uh, ouch."

They all laughed.

"Give me directions, and we can pick up your bags now," Deborah said, as she put the car in gear.

Half an hour later Deborah pulled into the drive of the home where she and Michael lived. She drove around Anthony's Porsche and pushed the garage door opener.

When they were parked inside, Anthony helped Deborah get Michael out of the car and into the house.

Michael reached Anthony' chest at the same spot as Janet did. Although five foot seven inches was considered tall for a woman, it was average too short for a man. But he'd proved his stature made no difference to his bravery.

"Make yourself at home, brother."

Warmth filled Anthony at the welcome. "I will. And thanks."

*There is a friend that sticketh closer than a brother.*

How true the verse was. After what he and Michael had been through together they were bonded tighter than blood relatives.

# CHAPTER 16

"Thanks for everything, Deborah. I need to touch base with my wife before I turn in for the night." Anthony dreaded having to tell Becky about the latest spiritual battles. But, surely she would be as excited about the victory God was giving, as he was.

"It's no problem." Deborah opened a kitchen drawer. "I have the key to the guest suite in here somewhere." She found and handed it to Anthony. "Just follow the stone path to the left after you go down the front steps."

He took the key, and with his duffle bag in tow, he followed his hostess's directions, making a left turn onto the stone walk.

As he approached the door of the guest suite and reached for the handle, he was aware something evil stood between him and the door.

Anthony stepped back. There was no moon out, and with the sky being overcast, he had a little difficulty seeing the entrance.

A stranger appeared and thrust a knife toward Anthony. "Why have *you* come here?"

"Time to do battle," God whispered to Anthony's heart.

Out of the corner of his eye, Anthony saw a

figure slipping through the darkness around the nearby trees. Was this yet another enemy? Was he surrounded? He would not turn to look. *God are you still there?*

Then he heard a small, low voice and recognized it immediately. His sister, Janet stood behind him.

"I am here. I have given Janet the vision to come help you," God again spoke to Anthony in his heart.

He had known for a long time his sister held strong connections to the Lord, but was amazed that Janet was indeed ready to join the team.

"Are you afraid of him?" He whispered to his sister, nodding toward the dark stranger.

~*~

Janet trembled. "Yes," she admitted. "But now that school is out, the Holy Spirit told me it was time to join you. He was perfectly clear about it all in a dream."

"Call upon Jesus' name, then, and say you will not be afraid."

Janet trembled. "I will not be afraid." Her voice was squeaky, and she took a step backward.

"No." Anthony put his hand on her shoulder. "You have to say His name and speak boldly."

"In Jesus name, I will not be afraid." Janet responded loudly but shakily.

Immediately the full set of armor descended upon her body. It was complete with sword, shield, and helmet, with her new name written on her right upper arm *Faith-Woman.*

"Janet," the Spirit spoke to her heart. "You have known me since childhood. You are now a warrior. No more fear."

At that moment Janet felt strength fill her which she had never known.

"You little coward," Amaros, the demon spirit mocked her. "You would like to seem brave, but you are nothing but a cup filled with trembling."

He threw his head back and laughed. Then he lifted the dagger in his hand.

"Janet, fear not, I, the Lord your God, am with you," the Holy Spirit spoke once more.

Janet lifted her sword as well, and the dark stranger turned to run into the darkness.

"Oh, no, lying spirit. You will be destroyed this night." With one swipe of the sword, Janet cut the legs out from under the demon, and he rolled to the ground, cursing and screaming.

"You are finished, demon of Fear. I will not need to battle you again. Not one more day."

Amaros attempted to throw his dagger at Janet but her fear had turned to Trust. The blade flew through the air and landed uselessly at her feet.

The conquered demon disappeared.

Janet turned to her brother. "It's gone."

"Yep, you fought the Good Fight." Anthony hugged her tightly. "I'm so glad to see you. Welcome to the team. You did great."

"No, the Holy Spirit did great"

"Well, yeah, but you stood strong."

~*~

"Hey, I thought I heard something out here. Is everything okay Anthony?" Another voice penetrated the darkness.

"Oh, sure, Deborah. Meet my sister, Janet. She's come to join me."

Ever the perfect hostess, Deborah smiled and held out her hand. "Hi, Janet, welcome. Will you stay the night? We have an extra bedroom inside."

Janet shook Deborah's hand. "That would be wonderful. Thanks so much. Will I meet Mr. Reeves tomorrow?"

"Sure." Deborah nodded. "How about we visit with the two of you in the morning over pancakes and sausage?"

"Wow, sounds great." Anthony laughed.

"I knew you would say that." Deborah rolled her eyes and turned back to his sister. "Come on inside, Janet. Let's get you to your room."

As the two middle aged ladies walked arm-in-arm down the path, Anthony picked up his duffle bag again.

*Maybe now I can get some rest. It has been a long day.*

Once inside the guest suite, Anthony called Becky. The phone rang and rang. He was about to give it up when Ben answered.

"Hi Dad."

"Why aren't you in bed?"

"I was. I am. Mom brought me the phone."

"Does that mean she's not talking to me?"

"Guess so. Do you know where Aunt Janet went?"

"Yes, I just saw her tonight. She ended up here in Ohio with me."

"Dad, I haven't forgotten my promise to pray for you. But now Mom thinks if she goes to church she will have to fight monsters, and"

Anthony winced. "Okay, slugger. I'll keep praying for both of you as well."

After he rang off, he climbed into bed and tried to settle down, but sleep came fitfully during the first few hours.

He was torn between depression over his family and excitement over the coming days. God had told him He would be adding more members to the team.

He knew the quest before them would be daunting but Anthony would be ready.

## CHAPTER 17

Sunday morning dawned bright and beautiful as only an Ohio day in late June can do.

Anthony and Janet sat at the table with their host and hostess and enjoyed the delicious pancake breakfast, Deborah had promised. And Anthony filled them in on the news that the Holy Spirit had added a new member to their team.

"Wow." Michael exclaimed after Anthony walked him through the past night's events, moment by moment concluding with the final victory scene.

"Janet, I am amazed at the battle you and Anthony fought while I slept peacefully in my bed. Welcome to the team. You did great."

"Well, like I told my brother—I was so afraid in the beginning. But with God's help I felt confident by the time I delivered the final blow. It was definitely the Holy Spirit who directed the fighting."

"I'll have to admit I'm glad God just expects me to be you guy's support system," Deborah said.

Anthony held up his hand. "Make no mistake. We need all the support people we can get." How he wished Becky was one of those support persons. He didn't dare tell Janet how her leaving New York had thrown a wrench in those plans.

"I need to check out the local churches," Janet said. "Do you have any suggestions, Deborah?"

"I don't. We need to find a church too."

"Since Michael is still recuperating, we'll just worship together here today," Anthony said.

And then the men began to tell Janet of the spiritual battle they had fought the day before while she traveled the roads between New York and Ohio.

Janet took a deep breath. "I have a feeling I arrived just in time to help on something big."

"So how does all this work. Do we each have to fight a demon before we are on the team?"

"Well, the first step is to become a Christian. And, Janet, in your case," Anthony touched her forearm. "You have been one for a long time."

Anthony paused for a moment. "And God gave me my armor before I had to fight."

"I'd like to know more about this myself," Michael inserted. "When was the first time God gave you the armor? Did it look just like when you fought the Panther here in the living room?"

"Actually God gave me the armor for the first time when I first met you, Michael. You couldn't see it because you were not yet a believer."

"Why did you need the armor then?"

"Michael your room was filled with a dark and evil presence. A twisted beast with two heads."

"Really? What did it do?"

"You know, I wish you could have witnessed it.

But I am sure your time is coming. Mastema presented himself as what I call it a Siamese twin of Hate and Fear."

"Yes. That is the emotions I felt," Michael said.

"I ran off Mastema with the name of Jesus and spiritual songs but I knew it was just temporary. Sure enough he came back the next day and caused you to pull the gun on us."

"I wish I could go back and rewind that part of my life."

"No. God has a way of using even our bad experiences for good once we accept Him as our Lord and Savior."

"Why couldn't I see your armor?" Deborah asked. "Did you ever wear it around me?"

"Yes, God gave me the armor when I ran off Perdix, the demon of despair that was harassing you. He tried to drown you in your tears. If you didn't see the armor, God was protecting you."

Janet helped Deborah clean up after breakfast, and the four of them settled in the comfy chairs in the living room.

"What are you studying, Michael? We can read the chapter where you left off.

~*~

After a late and simple meal of cold sandwiches, Janet called Pastor Good.

"I just want to check in. I haven't had a chance to locate a church here in Ohio yet. The man at the place where Anthony and I are staying was injured yesterday so we stayed here and had home worship."

"Where do these people usually attend?" Pastor Good asked.

"I understand they are new to Christ, and they haven't found a place yet. I hope to help with that."

"Don't wait too long to connect with a local congregation," Pastor Good admonished her. "Remember that the devil walks around like a roaring lion."

"That's right. We can feel it too. He is trying to devour as many of us as he can."

# CHAPTER 18

After Deborah left for her job at the day care on Monday morning, Anthony and Janet sat at the table with Michael and lingered over another delicious breakfast.

Michael glanced at his hands. "I have to go by the hospital and pick up some paperwork before my court appearance. I know this isn't going to be a fun time, but I have to face all that I have done."

"Not to worry, brother, God has plans for all of this. He makes good what Satan means for harm," Anthony said "I'd like to go with you and bring Janet along as well, if that's okay."

Michael beamed. "I would love it. I'm not sure I should be driving yet anyway."

"I better tell the two of you God informed me to expect another battle today," Anthony said.

"I thought we might have a break," Michael said with a shrug. "I'd hoped for a bit more time to heal."

"Really? Another battle? Did He tell you about it? Do you know any details?" Janet asked.

"Really, another battle," Anthony answered her first question then pushed back from the table. "Are we all ready?"

"With God all things are possible," Michael said.

"We have to be ready," Janet added. "We're a team now."

Anthony stood. "Well, let's go."

The other two stood up as well and followed him out the front door toward the car.

Arriving at the hospital, Anthony parked the Porsche.

"You go ahead and find the business office, Michael. I want Janet to meet another friend who works here."

Michael studied him for a moment. "Okay. Meet you in the cafeteria when I'm done."

He turned left and went down the hall.

Janet and Anthony kept walking in the direction that Michael's room had been before he was discharged.

The person Anthony remembered was standing at the nurse's station. "Hi, Abby."

Abby turned from a chart she was reading and smiled at him.

"Mr. Markson, good to see you again. And is this Mrs. Markson?"

He smiled. "No. But she is my sister, Ms. Janet Markson."

"It's nice to meet you, Abby." Janet took Abby's hand in both of hers. "I've heard such good things about you."

"Don't believe a word of it. It's this brother of yours who's a real mystery."

They laughed.

Hands tucked into his pockets, Anthony rocked back on his heels a bit. "I'm not much of a mystery but I do have a story for you."

Abby nodded to Janet "See, I told you. You never know what he's got up his sleeve."

"I've known him longer than you," Janet said with a laugh. "You don't know the half of it."

"Well, follow me to the break room," Abby whispered as though she were trying to be confidential, "We should have some privacy in there. And I was just thinking about another cup of coffee."

In the deserted break room, the three of them each filled a coffee cup and sat at a table,

Anthony explained what had happened to him since the day he'd appeared in Michael's room. Then they discussed the incident with the gun.

"Yes," Abby agreed. "Michael is an angry man."

Janet and Anthony looked at each other.

"Okay, you two," Abby said. "Tell me what's going on."

Anthony leaned forward a bit. "Actually, Michael has changed a great deal. He is now a man of great valor and integrity, and the Lord has called him."

"You're kidding." Abby's eyes widened. She smiled. "Isn't that wonderful." She took a breath. "But, called him? Called him to what?"

"To a team of warriors established to fight for

others whom God selects. He has called us to Spiritual warfare against demons."

"Amazing. I thought there was something very different about you the first day we met. I knew you to be a man of God, that's why I called you *brother*."

"Have you felt God might be speaking more to you? To your heart?"

Abby opened her mouth to speak but at that moment the door opened, and Michael stuck his head into the room.

"I thought you two might be back here," he said as he walked over to them. "Hey, Abby. Good seeing you again."

Suddenly the door crashed against the wall as another nurse marched into the room.

She looked at the four of them and then fixed her gaze on Abby. "I'm looking for Abby Power. Is your name, Abby?"

Abby nodded without saying a word.

"Well I'm your charge nurse for the day, and I've been told you spend a great deal of time on break. Maybe you don't realize it, but you only get one break between the beginning of your shift and lunch."

Abby's face reddened. "And your name is?"

"My name doesn't matter." The charge nurse tossed her head back. "I need for you to get back to your station, and as for the rest of you," she pointed to the team, "why are you in here? This is an employee break room and is not for visitors."

Anthony stepped toward the nurse, "We are so sorry, Miss"

"*Nurse* will do," she said emphatically.

She stretched out a long skinny finger and pointed it at Michael. "Mr. Reeves, you should be in jail by now."

Michael looked at her intently, "I don't believe you are a nurse." He started toward her.

Anthony gave a nod to Janet and then looked at Abby with a question in his eyes.

"Not a nurse? Why, Mr. Reeves, who are you to be deciding who I am?"

With a cackling laugh, the rather accusatory *nurse* began to morph into a spinning tornado. It came toward them, knocking chairs over and scattering tables against the walls of the room.

A full coat of armor began to cover all of them except Abby who wore only the breastplate she'd had before.

Abby stumbled backwards, terror on her face.

Swords drawn, Janet and Anthony stepped beside Michael and the three faced the whirlwind.

~*~

Abby observed how the others stood. Seeing their armor, she steadied herself and faced the whirlwind as well. "This is my battle. In the name of Jesus, our Lord, I demand that you depart."

"You." The spinning stopped leaving an ugly

haggard being in its wake. "You are nothing. Your mama was a drunk, and your daddy disappeared when you were a child," the demon Succumbus shouted at Abby.

"Neither of them wanted you or cared about you, and your Mama sold you out to whatever man came along."

Abby's heart felt so pained, as if it would break. She felt tears rushing to her eyes and lifted her foot to take a step back.

"Stand firm," Michael whispered,

"Abby, I love you. You are my child. You are a treasure to me beyond silver or gold. Fight the battle," the Holy Spirit spoke directly to her heart.

"What's it to you, demon of discouragement?" Abby spoke in a shaky voice. "Be gone. You will not accuse me again."

Abby was immediately armed with the full coat of armor and sword, with her new name written on right upper arm *The Discerner.* "The God who cannot lie told me I am a valuable child. His child. The child of the Living God."

She stuck the sword of the Spirit into Succumbus's heart.

Although she fell to the ground, the hag glared up at Abby arrogantly, pretending to be triumphant.

Abby answered the proud look by stomping on the demon's neck with her booted foot, and then using the silver toe to kick her several feet away.

The hag withered as the four team members approached her and used their swords to cut her into pieces.

The pieces became charred, as though burnt by a fire. Ribbons of smoke floated to the ceiling and soon disappeared.

Holding up their swords the team clicked them together in victory.

"Wow," Michael said. "That was our longest battle yet."

"Well at least none of us were hurt," Anthony said.

"Whew," Janet breathed.

"Hurrah." Abby jumped up and down and pumped her fists. "You don't know how long I have been dealing with that hag of discouragement. She has tormented me since I was a child."

"Well, if you join up with us, you won't have to fight anything alone again." Anthony gave her a teasing grin.

Abby scowled. "If? Look here, mister, I *am* one of you. So says the Holy Spirit."

"Well, He's the Boss," Janet said with a chuckle. "And I don't mean Anthony."

Anthony nodded. "I'm glad you accepted the call."

Then the four of them linked arms to pray.

"Father, God. Jesus, the Son. Holy Spirit," Anthony called out each name, "Thank you for bringing this team together and for Victory in You."

"Amen." the team said.

Michael opened his eyes. "Okay, team. What's next?"

"Next?" Abby glanced at each of them. "I for one have to get back to work."

"Yes, and I wonder what's waiting for me at the courthouse?" Michael added.

# CHAPTER 19

Michael approached the courthouse with trepidation. He didn't remember much about the accident, and he'd told his lawyer that from the beginning. He hadn't seen the elderly couple or the teenager who had died.

Still, he felt so bad for their families. He was met in the corridor by his lawyer and guided into the courtroom flanked by two policemen. He had been released from the hospital to go home on his own recognizance but knew he might be arrested today, depending on the arraignment situation.

As he entered the courtroom, there was no family of the dead present, and Michael breathed a sigh of relief. He acknowledged the families' lawyers and the judge.

As soon as one of the lawyers for the families opened his mouth, Michael realized he had been involved in something traumatic. The opposing lawyer definitely had many more facts than he did.

Michael learned the car that had been ultimately crushed against the tree had been driven by the teenager who ran into him head-on.

The couple, trying to miss the back of Michael's car had veered off the right side of the road and overturned.

When pictures of the scene were shown to the judge, Michael had to gulp down a lump in his throat He had not meant to hurt anyone.

Shame gripped his heart. *How could I have driven when I was drunk? What kind of a life have I been living?*

So deep was his grief that Michael barely heard his own lawyer when he presented more facts concerning the incident.

*I am a sinner, Lord. I deserve all that is happening to me.*

Then suddenly his lawyer patted him on the back. "Mr. Reeves, you can go for now but do not leave town. There will be a hearing at a later date for the three DUIs, but it was determined by the eye witness account and the highway patrol's documentation and investigation that you were not the cause of these accidents."

Michael shook his head. "I wasn't? How?"

"Didn't you hear? The teen veered out of his lane and ran into you head-on. The elderly couple's car overturned when it ran off the right side of the road into the ditch," the lawyer explained. "You were not at fault for any part of either accident."

"Really? I can't believe it."

"Don't get too excited now. You were drunk, and you will have penalties, maybe even serve time because this is your third offense. But the good news is you didn't kill anyone." His lawyer patted him on the back again.

"I didn't kill anyone. I didn't kill" Michael kept repeating the phrase as a mantra as he turned and walked through the courthouse doors and out into the sunshine. He wanted to dance up and down like a kid.

"Thank you, Holy Spirit. I will never drink again."

The paperwork Michael held indicated he would have to return and appear before the judge in two weeks to hear the penalty for the three DUI charges.

He figured they were giving him time to heal from his surgery. And for now he went home with a thankful heart.

~*~

That evening the team celebrated not only Abby's battle and the resulting addition of her to the team, but also Michael's good news.

"I could not give God enough praise for his goodness toward me," he exclaimed to the group. He took Deborah's hand in his. "I'm still reeling from the fact my sweet wife has stuck with me through all of my stupidity. All the abuse. I have been such an idiot."

"Hush now, Michael. You have been made right with God, and with me, through Jesus and the power of the Holy Spirit."

Michael smiled at her and squeezed her hand.

Anthony turned to his sister, "Janet, are you

planning to return to New York?"

"No, I think I would like to stay here a while. I'd like to make it a point to learn about this town and the people who live here," she replied. "I'd reached the highest level I could expect at the elementary school. And frankly I am ready to get out of the New York system. I thought maybe I'd look for something here."

Anthony's eyebrows rose slightly, "Really? Has the Holy Spirit spoken to you further?"

She smiled, "Not a definite message, but I feel we may be here for a while. Which reminds me, the guest suite has another bedroom so would you mind if I move in there? It has another small room that could be an office and might be useful for the team."

"Sure, that's a great idea." Anthony rose from the table. "I am now aware that The Lord is beginning to give us new names, just as in Genesis 35 when he changed Jacob's name to Israel. My team name is *Warrior.*

"Well done, brother." Janet held her hand to her chest. "And I have also been given the name of *Faith-Woman.* How about you Abby?"

"Yes, Janet, my team name is *The Discerner"*

"Praise the Lord for what He is doing with the team," said Anthony. "We still do not understand much about the real meanings behind our names, but I am sure the Lord will enlighten us."

# Awareness

Michael looked at the floor. "I wonder when He will give me a new name."

"I am sure the Lord has plans for you, do not worry that your name has not yet been changed. Friends, I believe the Holy Spirit has plans for all of us—more than we can even imagine. I will say goodnight for now because I need to spend some quiet time, reading my Bible and praying."

"Me, too," Michael agreed.

Anthony walked on to the guest suite. *It's good having Janet here. How could I ever think she was annoying?"*

How were Becky and Ben doing? Was there hope for their future together?

While he was anxious about Michael's situation, Abby had assured him God had spoken to her about it.

Meanwhile he was also pondering a visit home to see his family. He would go the moment he got confirmation from God that the timing was right.

Anthony was torn. For now, he decided to give Becky a call. When he keyed in the number, she quickly picked up the phone.

"Hello?"

"Hi, Becky, how are you?"

"Okay, I guess. Except that Ben is out of school, and I'd always depended on Janet. But how about you? Are you coming home soon?"

Anthony could hear the wistfulness in her voice.

"I hope so. I'm in the middle of a situation right now, but, as soon as I get the okay, I will be back. I miss you."

"I miss you too, Anthony. I want our family back together."

"I know. I do too, only I also want to do what God wants me to do and for this moment, it's to stay here."

Becky sighed. "Ben needs his dad. I need you."

"Soon, Becky. We'll talk again soon. I promise. I'll come home as soon as I can."

"Okay. But don't take too long, Anthony." Becky hung up the phone without saying 'I love you.' That was a first.

## CHAPTER 20

The next morning Anthony was out on his daily run when Janet moved her things into the other bedroom of the guest cottage.

It didn't take her long to unpack her bags and hang her clothes in the closet. If she was going to stay here as the Lord had indicated, she would need to bring the rest of her clothing and personal items from New York.

Janet took her computer to the adjoining office and set it on the desk. She plugged it in to save the battery and went online to see what employment options were available in the area.

Interesting. The local law enforcement division website was accepting online applications for several jobs. One was an administrative position. The Holy Spirit whispered to Janet's heart to apply, and she promptly obeyed.

With a sense of satisfaction Janet decided to go to the hospital to see Abby, only to find she had the day off.

Janet was able to get Abby's cell phone number from the on-call list posted just next to the station. She dialed the number and waited for Abby's answer.

"Hello?"

"Hi, Abby, this is Anthony's sister, Janet."

"Well, hi." Abby responded.

"I hope you don't mind me getting your number from the list at the nurse's station."

"Oh, no, of course not, Janet. Are you still at the hospital?"

"I'm just leaving."

"Wait there a moment. I have two hours to get some errands done. Would you like to ride with me and get some lunch while we are out?"

"Sure."

"Then stay right where you are, and I'll be there in fifteen minutes."

"Great." As Janet ended the call, she asked God to guide her in her conversation with Abby.

Her brother had guessed correctly about God speaking to Janet. Now she wanted to discuss it with her new friend Abby who was the newest member of the team.

In fifteen minutes Abby arrived in her Ford Escape and grinned widely as Janet climbed inside. "Hey, lady, good seeing you again. How is the rest of the team? The three of you are all I've been thinking about for the last two days."

"The rest of us are great. Michael got good news about the wreck he was involved in." Janet continued to tell Abby all she knew about the court appearance.

"Wow, they determined it wasn't his fault. That's great." Abby smiled.

"Yes, it is. However, you know this is still going to be a rocky time for them."

"Of course." Abby leaned closer and lowered her voice, "What are you saying exactly?"

"Well, there is a reason that Michael is probably going to jail."

"Because of the DUI?"

"Actually, it's more than that."

"Girl, what are you talking about? What have you heard that I haven't?"

"God spoke to me through a dream last night." Janet raised her eyebrows.

"Okay, let's hear it," Abby probed. "What's the deal?"

"Well, I dreamed Michael was in this restaurant. He was a waiter, no less. And he knew many of the people who were dining there."

"Yes?" Abby's pony tail bobbed as she snapped her fingers in a *hurry up* gesture.

"I'm getting to it. You see there was only one other member of the wait team who knew about the inner workings of the restaurant. But Michael, who was new to it all, had to ask a lot of questions and search for items."

"And" Abby leaned closer. "Go on"

"Well, Michael questioned the customers but they didn't like all the inquiries. Of course, they still expected him to serve them exactly what they wanted."

"How could he know if he didn't ask?"

"Exactly. Then God explained part of the dream to me and told me only one thing I needed to do. He said, 'Janet, Michael is going to a place of which he will not know anything. He will have someone working with him who knows everything about the place. Both of them will meet someone who needs help desperately, and no one but Michael will be able to give him an answer."

"And?"

"That's it. I don't know what it all means but I was hoping you might."

"Me?" Abby pulled back and blinked. "I haven't heard a thing."

"But you're part of the team, and I was hoping" Janet frowned. "Oh, dear. Then what could it all mean?"

Abby's green eyes sparkled. "I don't know but I bet God will let me know."

"How?"

"Now that I know about your dream, I will listen for His voice very carefully in the coming days. I will pray about nothing else," Abby promised. "We will find out the interpretation of the dream."

"That brings up another thing. I need to find a local congregation to worship with."

"Of course, you do." Abby nodded. "You must

come to church with me."

Their lunch at the airport was a delightful time and neither mentioned the dream again but Janet couldn't help but wonder what it could all mean.

~*~

A few days later Janet received an email which excited her, and then she learned God had spoken to Abby as well.

The two of them knew exactly what to do and called a meeting of the team at Deborah and Michael's house.

Once again Deborah had prepared a delicious meal. But the two young women could hardly wait until they finished eating to discuss this new situation.

"Okay, team, let's get started with our meeting," Anthony began. "First of all, I know God has been speaking to some of you as well as He has to me. And I believe God has been speaking to me about getting some things straightened out at home."

Everyone's eyes focused on Anthony.

"I have decided that since we have to wait for Michael's sentencing, I am going home this weekend to see Becky and Ben and wanted each of you to know about it and to expect my absence for a few days."

Michael shifted and looked at the floor.

"I was able to talk with Becky briefly last evening," Anthony continued. "She and Ben are going through a lot right now. Ben is out of school, and with Janet not around to lend a hand, Becky feels overwhelmed. So I wanted all of you to know the situation." Anthony stood there a few moments.

"Wise choice, Warrior," God spoke to his heart in a quiet voice.

Chills ran over Anthony's shoulders. He glanced at Abby. "My wife works at a prestigious dermatologist's office in New York. She works as an Esthetician and is highly respected. I'm wondering what type of job opportunities would be open for her type of work near Clanston."

Abby looked up. "I'll be glad to look into that for you."

Then Anthony turned to his sister. "Okay, Janet, let's start with your news."

"I have a job." Janet flicked a glance at Anthony. "So while you are in New York, little brother, you can pick up the rest of my clothing."

All eyes were on her as she continued with the news about the application to work in the law enforcement division just outside of Clanston as an administrative assistance and liaison between the local office and the state prison.

When she told the rest of the team about her dream their eyes widened.

"The Holy Spirit has spoken to me as well," Abby said excitedly. "I've been transferred to a nursing position at Clanston State Prison.

The team looked at each other in amazement.

"Michael." Abby waited until he looked at her. "Between Janet and I, you will not be alone should the judge give you jail time."

Michael leaned against his chair, and he could not hold back the tear rolling down his cheek. "Guys, I can't tell you how this makes me feel."

"The Holy Spirit spoke to me this morning on my run." Anthony put his hand on Michael's shoulder. "You *are* going to prison, but God's team has your back."

"Sounds like it," Michael said.

"You are going in there to help someone get free from his past hurts, habits and hang-ups. And you will influence many others to be free as well. Let's stay prayed up, team."

"Wow, I never thought I'd say this but I can't wait to get there."

They all chuckled at Michael's attempt to lighten the situation.

"I had my check up at the doctor's office today. He was amazed at the way my wound has healed. The stitches came out easily. And he said I wouldn't have much of a scar. But you know I expect a little one. I expect God will leave something to remind me of His goodness."

"Michael, I am glad for your healing, but still, you must remember, it won't be an easy stay," Anthony warned. "I can't even imagine how many demons will be in there."

They looked at each other with somber expressions.

# CHAPTER 21

The next day on his way to New York, Anthony prayed for increased wisdom where Becky and Ben were concerned. He knew God had called him to this work but how could he explain it to his family in a way they could understand?

"Spirit, speak to my heart about what to say and what not to say."

He knew more about how to explain all the things that the Spirit was doing for others and less how to explain the Spirit's influence in his own life.

It had been five weeks since his surgery. He'd only been given six weeks leave-of-absence. So some decisions had to be made, and soon.

He knew one thing. He was weary of the office politics at the large firm. More than weary of the frustrations and bad vibes that came from working for the type of clientele who brought in the big money. Truth to tell, Anthony had always wanted to have his own law practice, but until now he hadn't seen how it could happen.

However he couldn't go back. Not if he kept his commitment to God to be in Ohio. It was seriously time to find a position of some kind in his new location.

He shook his head to clear it. It seemed he had

been driving for hours, and the blackness of the empty road ahead hypnotized him.

Suddenly something loomed in front of his car.

Anthony slammed on the breaks, and his body lunged forward against his seatbelt. His head jerked backwards as the car came to a complete stop. He groaned from the pain in his neck and shoulder muscles.

As soon as he could manage to unlatch the seat belt, Anthony jumped out of the car. Vertigo caused him to grab the car door to steady himself.

Once the world quit spinning, he proceeded around to the front of the car. A man lay on the asphalt.

Anthony's heart seized in his chest. *I didn't hear a bump like I had hit anything, let alone this man. But I'm sure glad something caused me to stop when I did.*

A hat covered the man's head. Dark hands stuck out beyond his ragged and dirty coat sleeves. Even a tramp was valuable in the eyes of God. But he lay so still.

*Is he still alive?* Anthony moved closer to the victim and reached out his hand to touch his shoulder.

The moment Anthony's fingers touched him, the man jumped up with a gun pointed right at him.

Anthony winced and stepped back. He turned to run when he was met from behind by another man holding a knife and looking equally as ragged and dirty as the first.

"Hold it right there, mister. You're taking us for a ride." The voice of the man with the gun came from behind him.

The other man flashed his knife. "Get in the car," he growled, and motioned to the driver's seat.

Anthony got in as the man had ordered, and the transients climbed into the back seat.

"Drive," ordered the man with the gun.

"Wha—what's this?" Anthony stammered, "Where are we going?"

"Where were you headed?" the man with the knife waved it menacingly.

"Home," Anthony replied without thinking through the consequences of what he would say.

"Well," said the man with the gun. "Guess that's where we're going."

Anthony's heart dropped. Daylight was fading. It would soon be dark, and he was driving these guys home with him—where Becky and Ben innocently waited.

Anthony had driven what seemed like hours with the silent men riding in the back seat. He glanced in the rear-view mirror a few times just to make sure he had not dreamed the whole thing.

*Lord, I am getting so tired of these guns and knives. Maybe you could help me find a bullet proof vest?*

"Oh ye of little faith," God whispered. "Have you so soon forgotten?"

The next time Anthony glanced in the mirror, he noticed the man sitting in the back, behind the passenger's seat, was, not only wearing a hat but had grown a very long nose and a full head of shaggy hair now covered his ears.

Shape shifters. Demons from Malpas. He should have known. Anthony stomped on the break and pulled off the road. He got out of the car and opened the back door. "In the name of Jesus Christ, King of Heaven and Earth, the God whom I serve, get out of my car."

"No problem," the wolf in the hat said. "After all, we know where you live."

"Yeah." The other wolf snickered. "We've been watching your woman. Got her scared silly, we have."

"I claim the blood of Jesus over my family," Anthony roared. "Let them alone."

The wolf in the hat winced. "No need to holler. Yes, we have to recognize that for your son. But your wife will make her own decisions."

"That she will," the other wolf snarled.

As Anthony watched the wolves fade away he prayed. "God please protect my wife from her fears. Help her to know You. Why, why, why doesn't she recognize that closing her eyes to the spiritual world around us does not make it go away?"

## CHAPTER 22

After breakfast the next day, Ben went outside to play.

Anthony enjoyed another cup of coffee while he explained how Janet had found a job and planned to stay in Ohio. She needed him to bring the rest of her clothing. "Can you help me go over to her house and pack them?"

Becky turned her face away from him. "It's bad enough that you go off and leave without taking her away from us too."

"I didn't know she was coming until she showed up. But I have to admit I like it. I want all of my family to be with me."

She got up from the table and walked to the kitchen window. She was silent for a while, and he wondered what she was thinking.

Finally she turned to face him. "Anthony, I know you are not talking about me and Ben moving to Ohio. Surely you aren't talking about that are you?"

"Well, I can't see the problem. It's a nice enough town, and I'm sure we can find a house" his voice trailed off as he looked at her face. "What's wrong, Honey?"

"Anthony, we *have* a house. We would be

uprooting Ben from everything he is used to here."

"Sure there will be things Ben will miss, but kids are really flexible if they know their Mom and Dad love them.

Becky gave a very unladylike snort which he ignored.

"Janet will be there for him for this next school year, and you and I will be together and can start fresh in a new place."

"And my job. What about that? I guess it's not as important as your *calling*." Becky had her sarcastic tone perfected. "It seems this is what you always do. It's all about you."

"Becky, no. That is not the way I feel. Let me explain."

"I think you have said enough. I understand perfectly."

"No, Becky, you don't. I want"

"That's it. *You* want. It's always been about what *you* want." She turned from him and went to the back door, looking out at Ben.

Anthony came up behind her, placing his hands on her shoulders. He could tell she was truly upset by how tense she was. He felt her rejection.

"Becky, sweetheart. Please let me tell you about this."

He turned her around and embraced her. "I know things have not been right between us for a long time. I was not the husband I should have been. I want to ask you to forgive me."

He looked into her eyes and saw the hurt. "Can you do that?"

She was still and silent. Would she continue to resist him?

"I want us to start over. Will you at least think about it? I'll email you some information on the schools, and you can think about—if and when you want to give notice at work. God will guide us."

He hugged her to him, and then looking into her eyes, he asked again, "Will you at least think about it?"

She nodded.

He kissed her softly, and then let go of her and turned to the door.

"Ben?" He called and went outside to kick the ball with him.

~*~

She stood at the window looking at them playing and laughing with each other. Her blond Angelo husband and her mixed race son.

"Oh, God, help me," she whispered more to herself than to the God she didn't know.

"Anthony wants me to give up my job. I don't even know what's happening with his firm. Will they let him be gone so long and keep his position? And meanwhile I've been offered a raise."

She began to cry then. "How can I give up the only security I know while my husband goes and plays war games with demons?"

No answer. She hadn't expected one. It was up to her to keep things together.

Becky went into the bathroom and washed her face. Then she went out into the garage and found some empty boxes to pack Janet's things.

I wonder what Janet plans to do with her place? I suppose she will want me to keep checking it. As if I don't have enough to do already since she left me in the lurch. She and Anthony both left me in the lurch.

Becky kicked an empty box clear to the other side of the garage.

~*~

Anthony knew he'd said enough. He would have to prove he could support his family in Ohio.

After Becky helped him pack a few of Janet's things, small stuff, just what would fit in the trunk of the car, he took his family out for supper and to their favorite overlook of the city to see the fireworks.

Ben could hardly stay still. "This is so cool, Dad. This is the best fourth of July ever."

## CHAPTER 23

Janet was delighted Abby had invited her to go to church with her on Sunday. Pastor Good would be pleased.

When she drove her red Honda Civic into New Hope Trinity Church parking lot, it was almost full. *Must have an interesting pastor.* She found a space a couple of rows back and parked.

As she walked up the front steps, an elderly gentleman, standing just to the right of the large double doors, held one of them open for her. She nodded at him and smiled.

She entered the foyer, and immediately warmth and peace washed over her. This was very much like New Beginnings, her church back in New York. She mustn't forget to call Pastor Good and let him know she'd found a place to worship.

Janet walked into a vestibule where two welcoming gentlemen handed her a program of the service.

She glanced around the comfortably large sanctuary with beautiful stained-glass windows all along the sides of the walls. The room could easily seat two hundred people.

The lovely choir loft in the back was complete

with an organ on the wall of one side of the church and a piano on the other.

A beautifully carved podium stood on the pulpit in front of the room and held a huge Bible.

Janet recognized Abby from her long pony tail. She was sitting with another woman close to the front.

Abby saw her at the same moment and motioned for her to move up several pews to sit with her.

Janet did so and as she sat down, Abby reached over and squeezed her hand. "So glad you could come," she whispered.

"Beautiful," Janet whispered. She'd only missed one week, but still, it felt so good to be back in church.

The choir loft was full, and as the organist started the music, they began to sing, with voices harmonizing perfectly. Janet's heart swelled as she listened, her fingers itching to race across the ivories once more.

When the music finished and the choir was seated, an elderly gentleman stepped in front of the podium.

"I would like to welcome all our members and visitors to worship this morning. My name is Pastor Joseph Milton, known as Pastor Joe to most of you."

He glanced over the sanctuary "I'd like to thank all of you for your prayers these past few weeks during my illness. I am feeling better but as most of you know, I have turned the operations of our church over to Robert now. My son, Reverend Robert Milton will be preaching for us today. Please make him feel welcome."

The congregation clapped politely, and the reverend stepped to his father's side. He looked to be about forty years-old, blonde hair, slightly grey at the temples and a gracious smile.

"Thanks, Dad. And thank you to this congregation for allowing me to serve."

Janet heard little of the sermon after that. She focused on the man himself. Personable and good looking, she liked him instantly.

His beige suit fitted perfectly, and the light blue tie he wore enhanced his eyes. His voice was steady and strong but not too loud, and best of all, his smile was dazzling.

After the service Abby introduced Janet to her friend Erin Ludwig. She was another tall woman, about Janet's height. The gold flecks in her brown eyes twinkled as she greeted Janet.

"She works at the emergency room. And we've been friends forever."

"Are you eating lunch with us? Erin asked Janet.

"I'd love to. I still don't know my way around this town."

Abby linked arms with her two friends. "You will love our favorite restaurant."

Reverend Robert greeted each one at the door as

they left, and when it was Janet's turn, he took her hand in his and asked her name.

She looked up into his face and found his blue eyes, framed by small laugh-lines, fastened on her.

He glanced past her at Abby, "Good morning, Abby. You didn't tell me you were bringing such a lovely friend with you this morning."

Janet blushed. He wasn't all that much younger than she was.

"You know I don't tell you everything, Reverend," Abby teased.

During the short walk to her car, Janet could feel his gaze resting on her. When she turned before climbing into the front seat, he stood where he'd been. He lifted one hand and gave her a brief wave.

Minutes later the three women sat at a table in a nearby café for lunch.

Abby glanced at Janet before she picked up the menu. "How did you like the service?"

"It was wonderful. The church was gorgeous," Janet answered. "And the pastor was nice."

"Pastor Joe?" Erin raised one eyebrow.

"Yes, him, too."

And they all laughed at Janet's answer.

"Now I can call Pastor Good back in New York and let him know I have found a church home."

~*~

Anthony took Becky and Ben to visit New Beginnings church.

# Awareness

Pastor Good welcomed them warmly. Anthony told him Janet had found a job in Ohio and would be staying with him for a time but that his family, Becky and Ben needed a church home. He asked the pastor if he would watch over them while he was gone.

By the look Becky gave him, he could tell she was not impressed. He knew she thought he should be staying in New York himself.

But his calling was in Ohio. He sighed. Why couldn't she see that she needed to support him?

Anthony's prayer after the lights were out Sunday evening, was, "Lord, please don't let the things those shape-shifter wolves said rattle me." Then he shook his head, "*What am I thinking? God always works things out to those called to His purpose.*"

## CHAPTER 24

Before Anthony left for the long drive back to Ohio, he asked Becky and Ben if they could pray together, as a family.

Ben's answer was his usual "Yay." but Becky merely nodded. They gathered on the couch and Ben crawled onto Anthony's lap.

"Lord, I don't know exactly what you are doing with our lives. And I guess I don't really need to know ahead of time, but please give us all peace about it. Take care of Becky and Ben while I am gone, protect them, and help them both to understand why I have to go. Lord, I ask for traveling safety on the way back to Ohio. Our lives are in your hands, the best hands I know."

Becky was quiet as Anthony closed his prayer but Ben asked, "Dad, can I pray to God too?"

Anthony looked across the top of Ben's head and caught Becky's eye.

"Sure, son," he said.

Once again Ben bowed his head. "God, don't let Dad get in any accidents, and help Mom not to worry and cry when he leaves. Amen."

Becky managed a smile. "Thanks Ben."

~*~

# Awareness

Anthony knew Becky needed security. Although he'd always wanted to have his own law firm, up until now it had just been a dream. He'd have to admit he'd become complacent because he had done well at the old firm where he'd become a senior partner.

But in three and a half weeks, on July 29 and July 30 the nationwide state boards testing would be offered. If he didn't take the Ohio state boards then, he would have to wait until February.

And it was time to move on. After all, his leave of absence had ended, and he knew he couldn't go back. He'd need to call and tell them his decision.

It was after midnight when Anthony pulled up at Michael and Deborah's place and drove around to the guest house.

All was quiet as he walked the path.

When he unlocked and opened the guest house, he noticed Janet's bedroom door was closed. He carefully set down three boxes full of the items Becky had packed.

Then he went back out to the car and brought in another load. As he took the box of law books into the office, Anthony hoped he'd brought the right ones. A lot of his new friends were asking for legal advice, and of course, he wanted to brush up for the coming exams.

Last, he brought in his luggage, and quietly put his bags down in his room. Then, removing only his shoes, he stretched out on the bed.

"God, thank you for a safe trip. Now that I'm back, help me to find some job opportunities that will interest Becky. Please, by the power of your Spirit, let Becky understand what You mean to me. What this team means to me. Bless the team and help us know what to do next."

~*~

Two weeks later Michael appeared for his hearing and was taken into custody.

He couldn't believe it had come to this. But he was to serve six months in the very prison for which Abby and Janet now worked. Michael glanced around but didn't get a glimpse of either of his team mates.

At first he felt let down. But he'd surrendered to God, and the Lord God had promised to be with him. He remembered how Anthony had talked about the Lord having a job for Michael to do. But what in the world could he accomplish locked up in this gloomy place?

As he passed each cell, demons made themselves known. Some did little more than whimper but many screamed and howled.

It was with relief that Michael finally reached an open cell door where Warden Tate waited for him to enter.

There was nothing in the cell but a bunk bed, lavatory, and a commode, and of course, his cellmate.

This guy could not have been more than 20 years-old, if that. He was a bit taller than Anthony, and at five foot seven inches, Michael had to look up at him. With his olive complexion and slightly hooked nose Michael pegged him as of Jewish decent.

He cautiously nodded at his cellmate, but the man continued to stare glassy eyed as though looking straight into Michael's soul.

Michael placed his Bible on the top bunk. It was the only thing he'd been allowed to bring here and then only after it had been searched thoroughly.

Lying on his bed that night, Michael was subjected to hours upon hours of yelling, screaming, crying, and words of rage. When one voice would trail off, dozens of others would begin.

And it was so cold no matter how he wrapped himself in the threadbare covers, he could not get warm. His bones ached.

There was no light at all. The darkness in the cell block was blacker than anything he had ever endured.

Michael had never had such a disturbing experience as he had that night. He would be glad when morning came.

~*~

Daily, ever since he'd returned from New York, Anthony prayed that Becky would agree to at least consider moving to Ohio. "*What will I do if she doesn't?*"

When he analyzed all the things that had happened to him since he'd been staying in the guest house, he knew God had called him here. He had met some great friends, but more than that, God was building a team, and they now had four team members.

God was working tremendously in their lives, but still, Anthony missed his family.

Maybe tonight he'd give Becky a call and see if she was any closer to making a decision about moving. He could even start looking for a place to set up a law office. No. He'd call her all right, but no pressure. He'd keep it friendly and superficial.

*I better not rush things. I've not even taken the Ohio board exams yet. I'll just pray and check into the situation. What if I don't pass the first time? What if I have to do something else to make a living in the meantime? When I have something more to offer, I'll ask her then.*

## CHAPTER 25

For Michael, morning only brought more discomfort. More pairs of eyes staring straight through him. More eyes in the halls going to and from the showers as well as in the cafeteria.

The food was bland, and Michael was unsure of what most of it was.

Then, lined up like animals, the inmates proceeded back to the cells and were, once again, locked away.

Back in his cell, Michael grabbed his Bible, and slid down the side of the wall of his cell. He sat on the floor and began to read.

His cellmate flushed the toilet and sat down on the floor as well, on the opposite side of the room. The guy's eyes were a little clearer today.

"What are you reading?" he asked.

"The Bible," Michael answered quietly.

"Well, I know that," the man retorted sarcastically. "Which book?"

"You've read the Bible?" Michael answered the question with another question of his own.

"Well, my old lady read it to me when I was little. Nonsense mostly, but she made me listen."

"Good for her, but it's not nonsense."

"Says who?" The other man's lips curled into a

scowl.

Michael shrugged. "Well, I believe it. And your Mama must have believed it, too."

"Oh, yeah. She was one of those church-going people. You know how they are. All the time it was 'Get ready for church.' 'Time for church.' 'Hurry we'll be late for church.' It was a royal pain."

"So you went?"

"Had to. The old man didn't go, and I knew what I would get if I stayed home with him."

Michael noticed his cellmate was beginning to sweat, shake, and rub his hands. He was probably in withdrawals from whatever he'd been using.

"Hey, you okay?" Michael asked.

"Not really." his cellmate drew his knees up and dropped his head over on them.

"Guard," Michael yelled.

"Shut up," the guy ordered. "Don't call anyone. It's more trouble than it's worth."

"You sure? Hey, what's your name? I don't even know what to call you."

"Josh. I'll be okay."

However, in just a few moments, a guard got their attention by running his baton against the bars of their cell. "What's happening in here?"

"Nothing," Josh bellowed.

"I figured as much," the officer replied sarcastically and walked away.

When Michael glanced at Josh again, a scaled

claw with sharp talons was wrapped around his cell-mate's chest.

"Botis," a voice whispered.

Michael stood up in alarm at the demon's manifestation.

*Will my armor work in here?* Immediately he became aggravated with himself. *What am I thinking? The Holy Spirit doesn't just abandon anyone.*

When he looked over at the cell door, Abby was standing beside it. She put her finger to her lips to signal for Michael not to say anything as she quietly unlocked the door and entered.

"Josh," she whispered.

He glanced at her with a troubled countenance. By now, it wasn't only his hands shaking, but rather his whole body trembled.

She turned and called for the guard again. He came fairly quickly at the sound of the nurse's voice.

"Help me get this man to the infirmary," Abby said with authority.

The guard lifted Josh off the floor.

Abby followed them out of the cell. She locked the cell door behind her, glancing at Michael, as she did. She gave him a nod and turned back to her patient.

~*~

Once in the infirmary, Abby called to report the situation to the doctor and took his order.

She found the medication Josh needed and started an IV.

He began to improve within the hour and was resting more comfortably as Abby's shift ended.

She turned her keys over to the incoming nurse and checked out as usual, going through the front of the prison.

The officers, checking her through the metal detector, were chatting about where they were going after work, and then one of them spoke directly to her. "Hey, nurse, where do you go for fun after hours?"

She turned to see a blonde-haired man with a nice smile. Almost too good looking, he was about her height with a name tag which read Tadd James. *What was that saying? Never trust a man with two first names.*

"Home to Grizzly," she answered with a smile of her own. "My Rottweiler," she added, and continued walking to the parking area.

Abby couldn't help thinking about Josh much of the evening as she dined alone at her apartment with Grizzly at her feet. The man was a looker, likely a heart breaker. Not tall dark and handsome as the saying goes, but blonde hair, blue eyes and a dazzling smile would go a long way in her book.

The Holy Spirit spoke to her heart quietly as she ate.

She bowed her head, "Yes, Lord," she answered.

# CHAPTER 26

Abby's phone rang early the next morning. Caller ID indicated Deborah was calling.

"Morning."

"Hi, Abby. Have you seen Michael?"

She detected a little anxiety in Deborah's voice.

"Sure have, honey. He's okay. He is right where God needs him to be."

A sigh of relief came through the phone. "Thanks, Abby. You'll never know how glad I am that you are there."

"You're welcome, honey. I'm glad too." Abby ended the call and then prepared for work.

About an hour later she was again going through the metal detector.

She greeted the officers. Then she took the sidewalk to the prison dorms and passed through each locked door using her ID card.

As she approached the infirmary, Abby reached for her key, but noticed the door was slightly ajar. *That's unusual.*

Pushing the door open with her shoe, Abby saw her relief nurse lying on the floor with blood in her hair. Josh stood over her.

"Guards!" she screamed.

Josh looked up with terror filled eyes.

The injured nurse moaned.

Abby knelt down beside the woman and examined her wound. "It looks superficial but I'm going to call the doctor. It won't take him long to get here. Please just lie still."

The nurse whispered something.

"Do you know who did this?" Abby asked.

"I didn't do it." Josh pleaded, holding up his hands in protest.

But the guards surrounded him and grabbed his arms. "Let's go."

Abby looked into Josh's eyes then down at his hands. "Wait," she said to the officers.

She glanced around the area looking for a discarded weapon as she moved toward the cabinet to get her flashlight. Then she returned to Josh. "Open your eyes."

After she examined his pupil's reaction from the flashlight, she turned to the guards.

"Okay, officers, you can take him back to his cell, but the doctor needs to see him later."

Her eyes met the guards. "He didn't do this. Whoever hurt her still has the weapon, and he's probably hiding somewhere."

The guards nodded at her as they took Josh away. "Okay, nurse. Your call."

Then the prison was put on lock-down, and a crew of officers began to search the entire prison.

# Awareness

Abby was cleaning the injured nurse's wound when the doctor arrived and sent the nurse/patient to another room for further treatment.

~*~

Meanwhile, back at the team's office, Anthony called his law firm in New York.

"Dickerson, Markson, & Clark," Miranda answered.

"Hey, Miranda. Anthony Markson here."

"Anthony. We've all missed you. Are you healed up yet? I thought you were coming back last week."

"I'm better," Anthony said cautiously. "Is Mr. Dickerson in?"

The silence was deafening.

"Miranda?"

"Oh, yes, let me patch you through."

"Dickerson."

"Markson here."

"Have you made your decision?"

"Yes. I still can't leave my situation here in Ohio. So go ahead and process my severance clause with the terms we agreed upon last week."

"Sorry to see you go, Markson. You were a real asset to the firm."

"Thank you, sir, I appreciate that."

"And all your banking information is correct?"

"Let's go over it to make sure," Anthony said.

When the Ohio bank routing was confirmed Anthony rang off.

He felt a great weight lift from his shoulders. Now he just had to make sure he was scheduled for the Ohio Bar exam. The timing was good because the exam was only given twice a year and the next date was less than two weeks off.

~*~

It was lunchtime before Abby was able to check on Josh again. When she got to his cell, he and Michael were talking in a serious and low tone.

"Hi, guys. Josh, I came to see if you were okay."

She saw Michael close the Bible that was on his lap.

"Are you all right?" Michael asked.

Josh looked back and forth between the two, puzzled.

"Sure, I'm fine."

Then Abby glanced at Josh, "Feeling okay?"

"I'm good." Josh looked sheepishly at her. "Thanks for standing up for me."

"Just doing my job. The doctor will take a look at you later, and then you may have to be processed to clear yourself."

Abby looked from one man to the other. "You guys better get ready for another wonderful meal, but at least you get room service today since we are on lockdown, and they are still searching for the person who hurt the other nurse."

She unlocked the cell door.

~*~

# Awareness

As Abby stepped out the door, Michael saw a greenish-brown blur slide past her and grab onto Josh.

Josh gave a muffled scream as he was dragged through the partially opened cell door.

Michael jumped up, certain Josh would be harmed if they didn't help him in some way.

Josh had already been implicated in an assault, and now something was trying to destroy him.

"Do not fear. It is time for My Warriors to do battle," God spoke to Michael in that moment.

Michael's armor covered him, and his sword gleamed at the end of his hand. "But God, I'm a prisoner here."

"Never forget. You are here by My hand. Do not fear, I have given you the gift of Wisdom," the Holy Spirit spoke clearly and audibly. Michael's new name, *The Shrewder*, appeared on his upper right arm.

Abby was also clothed in armor.

Together *the Discerner* and *the Shrewder* stepped out of the cell and into the hall.

Michael glared at the creature holding his cellmate. They were up against a gargantuan dragon, with apparently impenetrable greenish-brown scales covering his body. The legs and feet were massive, and its head reached the ceiling.

The raging dragon roared and fire shot out of his mouth.

Michael felt the heat and threw his shield of faith up in front of him. As soon as the fire diminished, Michael wielded his sword and stuck the end of the silver blade into-the only part of the dragon's body that was exposed—the throat.

Blood spurted out in all directions. However, the monster still held Josh tightly with a massive arm. Both of his hands tapered into sharp claws of steel, and one claw remained near Josh's neck.

Abby stood beside Michael with her sword drawn. And then Janet, as *Faith-Woman*, stepped out of the shadows.

She bravely came behind the dragon, fully ready for battle. She leaped toward the massive tail that switched from side to side. With one chop, Janet used her sword to slice through the tail. The dragon roared, twisted his huge head, and sent fire toward her.

Her shield went up. She moved to the other side of the dragon and shoved the blade of her sword completely up to the hilt into his fleshy underside.

The dragon twisted in the opposite direction and loosed Josh who plunged to the floor.

All three warriors continued to wield their swords until the dragon had collapsed and disappeared.

All that remained was a large Asian man lying on the prison tile. He didn't seem to be injured but he was definitely unconscious. Evidently knocked out when the dragon fell on him.

# Awareness

When Josh tried to stand, he couldn't. He was bleeding profusely now and obviously going into shock.

Abby, back in her usual nurse's uniform, put hand pressure to a wound on his chest.

Michael dressed in his prison jumpsuit moved quickly into the cell.

"Guards." Abby yelled. "Get an ambulance. We've got a serious situation—this man has lost a lot of blood."

Michael threw a thin blanket to Abby.

She grabbed it and knelt over Josh again, applying pressure to his chest.

One of the officers made a call, and an ambulance was there in just minutes.

As they loaded Josh on the gurney and rushed him toward the ambulance, Abby waited for the two other officers running toward her.

"Come get this guy. He's probably your perp." She gestured to the huge Asian man covered with tats of all kinds, lying on the floor behind her.

When they began to move the man, one of them picked up a hand-made knife by his side.

"Hey, that's Big Jax from the other cell block downstairs," one of them said.

"He must have broken out this morning during shower time and forced his way into the infirmary. Wow, how did you subdue him, nurse?"

Abby turned to them and shrugged. "I guess

somebody was looking out for me." She began to walk toward the infirmary, then stopped at Michael's cell and looked at him with a worried expression. "Josh is hurt pretty badly."

Michael held up his Bible. "I guess that means its prayer time."

Abby nodded, "Isn't it always? I haven't stopped praying since I walked into the prison this morning."

After the others left, Michael sat on his cell floor pouring over his Bible. He was reading in Revelation, Chapter 9, which spoke of demons coming up out of the pit in the last days and hurting people.

He thought about all the creatures the team warriors had fought so far, and how the demons had attempted to kill them and to interfere with the gospel going out to others.

There was so much he needed to know but there were not enough hours in the day to study his Bible to learn. He had to pray for discernment.

However Michael's heart overflowed with joy, because his name was finally changed. He was at peace as he prayed for his new friend Josh and finished with praise. "Thank you, God, for your Spirit, who speaks with us and gives us warnings and wisdom."

~*~

When Abby's shift ended, she drove straight to

the hospital and joined Janet who had arrived moments before her.

They learned Josh had arrived at the hospital in critical condition, barely conscious from the loss of blood. His chest wound was deep, and after a quick exam by the doctor in the Emergency Department, he'd been taken immediately to surgery.

Janet called Anthony, and he was soon on his way to the hospital as well.

The three huddled together to pray as they waited for the doctor to come to the waiting room and give them a report on Josh.

"Here he comes," said Abby.

"Are you the group waiting for word on Josh Pennington?"

"Yes we are."

"Your man has bruising to his heart and a collapsed lung. We are taking him to ICU, and a team of doctors will manage his case around the clock."

## CHAPTER 27

For the next few days Janet and Abby had taken turns going by to see Josh on their lunch hours and after work.

Anthony was in and out of Josh's room all day.

The fourth morning after the surgery Anthony sat beside Josh's bed when he opened his eyes.

"Who are you?" Josh asked in a weak voice.

"A friend." Anthony remembered saying the same thing to Michael not too long ago.

Josh just looked at him, then over at Abby and Janet. "You two helped save my life. Thanks." He closed his eyes and was soon asleep again.

The three quietly left the room, walked together down the hall, and took an elevator back to the entry area.

In minutes they were on the ground floor. Janet headed out. "I have to get back to work. How about you, Abby?"

"Yep, I'm on my way." Abby followed her out into the sunlight.

Anthony trailed behind the women. "Wait up."

The girls turned, and he motioned for them to wait for him. As he approached, they gathered close.

# Awareness

"Warriors. I am so excited about this calling and to have the two of you with me. Now we are seeing God work in Josh Pennington's life. Let's pray for him this night."

~*~

Josh woke up the next morning and instinctively tried to sit up on the bed. That was a mistake. Pain surged through him, and he lay back down.

Glancing around, he felt on the side of the bed for the call button. He pressed it once, twice but when he got no response he jabbed at the button over and over until a nurse entered the room with a cup of medicine.

"What do you need, Josh?"

"When am I getting out of here?" He tried to sit up again but made no more progress than before. "Is that something for pain?"

"It's your antibiotic but I can get you something for pain. I just need you to tell me your pain level."

"About 100," he blurted.

"No." She laughed gently. "You need to tell me between zero and ten with zero being no pain and ten being the worst you've ever had or can imagine."

He frowned. "Well then, it's still 100."

"Sounds like you are hurting too bad to go home soon."

The gleam in her eye and a shake of her head told Josh she was trying to scare him into being more cooperative.

"No, but, I guess if you knew home means jail for me, you might think I would not want to go," he shared with her quietly. "But I really do because I have got to talk to my cellmate as soon as possible."

The nurse walked over to him and gave him the antibiotic and a cup of water.

"Well, there are rumors that you might get to break out of here soon." She patted his forearm. "The doctor will be in to see you momentarily so lie back down and rest. I'll bring back something to help your pain in a few minutes."

Josh tried to relax but he didn't go back to sleep. His mind raced as he waited for the nurse to return with some pain killer.

As he processed everything that had happened in the past few days and thought about the dreams he remembered, he knew he had to get back to talk to Michael soon.

~*~

The next afternoon the doctor allowed Josh to return to the prison.

But when he got there, Michael wasn't in their cell. Discouraged, Josh lay down on his bunk and the movie of his life played through his mind. Raised in poverty with an angry father, he'd finally rebelled. Now, here he was twenty-years-old, sitting in a prison cell.

Fear crept over his flesh. Why had Big Jax attacked him? Would he die by his hand in this very prison?

He was not ready to die. And this place was certainly not where he wanted to be for the rest of his life. And yet, what could he do about it? Where did he want to be? How could he rise above this life?

Drowsiness crept over him and he closed his eyes. After what seemed only minutes, a voice stirred in his unconsciousness, and Josh opened his eyes.

"Hey, you're here," Michael greeted him. "Abby thought you might be back today."

"Yep, it's me. 'Ya miss me?" He yawned.

"Me? Ah. Let me see now." Michael patted him on the knee. "Yeah I did, come to think of it. How are you feeling?"

"Hurtin' some, but I'm okay."

"I've got a lot to talk to you about."

"Yeah, well, I'm going to talk to you first. I need to know what happened in the hall the day I was injured."

"You don't remember?"

"I don't know if what I saw was real or just me coming down off drugs. Did I really see a dragon, or am I losing it? Who in the heck were those people who rescued me? One looked like you and—"

Michael's hand raised in the universal *wait* motion. "Whoa, ask one question at a time, friend. I might not be able to answer all of them at once."

"Well, look, I've been having dreams like you wouldn't believe. Someone talking to me. And a repeating song."

"Actually, I would believe," Michael interrupted.

"You would?" Josh's eyes widened.

"Yep, been there, done that."

"Really? What? When? Who?"

"Hey, you're doing it again. All the questions coming at once." Michael grinned. "Start at the beginning. Tell me about the dreams you had in the hospital and what you remember about them."

Josh rubbed his head. "I don't know if I was asleep, or if I was having visions and hearing voices, but I saw myself as a little boy."

"Okay."

"My mama rocked me and sang a song I used to hear in Sunday school about a guy named Jesus who loved me. A nursery rhyme, I guess." Josh looked at Michael to see if he was getting what he said.

He was encouraged as Michael nodded for Josh to continue.

"And then there was a Bible with a verse I learned from another Sunday school class about God loving the world so much He sent this guy, Jesus, to save it. I don't exactly know from what though. And then the horrible things my dad did to me. I don't think I can tell you all that, though."

"That's okay, Josh."

"I also saw my life as a teen—fighting with gangs for drugs, and there were guns and knives." He paused as he searched for just the right words.

"But then this voice. It was the kindest, most beautiful voice—but not a woman's voice—well this person told me I could be his child. Almost like I would have another Dad."

Josh broke into tears.

~*~

Michael kept his hand on Josh's back and let him sob. He knew how it felt. It wasn't long ago he'd been sitting in that same spot.

"It's the Holy Spirit," Michael said as Josh quieted. "He was speaking to you just as He spoke to me."

Josh's tear-drenched gaze fastened on Michael. "I don't know all about Him—the Holy Spirit—I mean—who is the same as God, the father and Jesus, the Son—but I will tell you all that I have learned in the past few weeks, and it is some pretty amazing stuff."

Michael continued to explain about God, the Holy Spirit, and Jesus who came to earth to die for our sins.

He explained how anyone can be forgiven if they ask Jesus, if they take on Jesus righteousness, then Jesus takes the person's sin on Himself, paying for the debt all sinners owe.

Michael had to stop several times to let Josh think about what he was saying and several times Josh's tears flowed again.

The two men talked well into the night, long after lights-out. Michael taught Josh a few of the

Bible verses he had come to love and read to remind himself of God's love for him.

Especially, he related to the one from Josh's Sunday school class about God giving His only Son to save us from having to pay for those sins and that He could do that because He had never sinned when He lived here.

Not only that, but whoever would believe in Jesus could live forever for Him now and be with Him forever when they died.

At last, Michael asked Josh if he believed.

"Oh yes," Josh replied. "I believe that Jesus died for me."

"Do you want to pray and ask Jesus to come into your life and become *the boss* of all you do or think or say?

"I sure do because I have made a mess of it. Why wouldn't I want the Person who knows it all to be in charge?"

"Good answer, my friend."

The two men bowed their heads. "Father, I have sinned and want you to come live in my heart. To be the boss of my life." Josh prayed a very simple prayer.

"Lord I thank you for my new brother. Comfort him in the days ahead. Strengthen us both for the work that you have for us to do," Michael prayed.

Later, as Michael was drifting off to sleep, he heard Josh say, "Oh, I forgot to ask you about the other day when I got hurt."

"Later, friend. Later. That's a whole other story."

Two believers slept well in the cell that night.

## CHAPTER 28

**B**ig Jax stared at the knife protruding from his belly. He was losing his edge and had to do something to reverse this lack of respect.

Things had gone from bad to worse ever since he'd failed in his mission to destroy that bastard Josh.

The demon Botis never gave up those who were his, nor did he tolerate failure.

~\*~

Earlier that morning, at the sound of the usual prison alarm for showers, Josh heard Michael roll out of his bunk.

But Josh laid there a second longer wishing he could sleep in for once. He groaned, rolled out, and soon joined his cellmate waiting for the door to be unlocked and to file into line.

*We go everywhere in a line here.* Since Josh was slow rolling out there was no time to ask Michael any questions before the line formed and they were headed down the hall toward the showers.

No sooner had they showered and dressed than Josh was called out by a guard who was to escort him to the infirmary.

"Hi, Josh," Abby said, as she met him at the door.

"Climb up here on the table so I can take off the dressing and look at your wound. The doctor wants a report first thing this morning."

Josh complied with Abby's instructions, and she checked him over.

"No drainage, surgical wound intact, I've put a clean dressing on this, and you've even got a twinkle in your eye. So as soon as you are dressed, you're good to go."

"Michael says Jesus put the twinkle in my eye." *Should he ask Abby about the war with the dragon?*

Just then another type of alarm blared throughout the prison.

"Nurse, please report downstairs to cell 202. Nurse to 202." Janet's voice came over the pager.

Abby picked up her bag and dashed out.

A guard named Tadd came to stand at the door of the infirmary while Josh was getting dressed. Josh had noticed him before but unless the prisoners stepped out of line the guards pretty much ignored them.

Josh finished dressing and was about to step over to the guard when the sound of screaming and cursing burst through the air.

The door was flung open, and another guard wheeled a gurney through the passage, banging this way and that.

Josh backed against the wall of the infirmary to avoid getting hit by the gurney. He felt evil sliding into the room along with the new arrivals.

Terror clutched his heart when he recognized his enemy, Big Jax, with a knife planted in the bottom of his abdomen.

When he saw Josh, he nearly came off the gurney, lunging at him in fury. "Your friends won't always be around," Big Jax growled. "You'll pay for turning your back on us."

~*~

Abby was soon on the phone talking to the doctor, and then she called the ambulance dispatch.

"We have an inmate who is wounded," she told the dispatcher. "He needs to go to the Emergency Department."

"We'll be there in five minutes, ma'am," The dispatcher replied.

"Be advised he is a large man and dangerous."

"Copy that."

"Even though he has a knife protruding from his lower abdomen and is experiencing much pain and discomfort, he has threatened one of the other inmates here. However, the wound does not have much bleeding. Vitals are okay at present."

"Copy," the dispatcher repeated.

The guards who had brought Big Jax to the infirmary were still trying to hold him on the stretcher even though he was strapped down.

"Ambulance is on the way," Abby informed them.

"Good." Tadd acknowledged her statement. "This

is one strong dude. They'll need some powerful anesthesia to hold him still enough to operate and get the knife out."

Josh continued to flatten himself against the wall until he found an opening. As soon as he possibly could, he sped out of there, almost beating the guard back to his cell.

"Whew." he exclaimed as he ran inside and slid to the floor. "Somebody stabbed Big Jax. The one they call the Dragon."

Two days later when Josh went to the infirmary to get his bandage changed Abby informed him Big Jax had been released from the hospital and returned to his cell.

That guy was bad news, and to think of him really unnerved Josh. He hoped he would never have to see Big Jax again.

## CHAPTER 29

**W**ith just a few months of his sentence left the warden agreed to let Josh help out in the infirmary a few hours each day. So Abby put him to work taking inventory of the first aid items.

"We need a better system to keep the stock rotated, so we can use up the older stuff first."

"Okay." Josh held up his notepad. "As soon as I get this list made out we can do some brainstorming."

"You got it. Just start with the shelving and drawers on the left side of the room and work your way around."

"Will do."

It was amazing what doing a meaningful job would do for a man. How much more beneficial it would be if this prison had a work detail for all the men. At least for the ones on good behavior.

Before long Josh was whistling.

"I didn't know you were musical, Josh. Do you know any hymns?"

"Michael and I have been singing Amazing Grace at night before we go to sleep."

"Cool. Let's sing it together." Abby hummed a

few bars, and then swirled around the room in a holy dance as she sang.

Josh whistled the tune to accompany her, but did his best to keep his mind on recording the inventory.

"Shut up the caterwauling," a deep voice bellowed.

The lights dimmed and went off.

Abby screamed.

Josh slowly rose from his bent position and glanced around.

Big Jax had Abby in a choke hold. "I'm hurting," he roared. "Where do you keep the pain medication?"

Josh tensed. He couldn't recall listing any pain medication on the inventory sheet.

Abby choked and gagged.

He had to do something. Josh let his eyes glance around the room again and tried to jog his memory. "I don't know where the pain stuff is, but if you don't quit choking Abby there is no way she can tell you anything, either."

"What's in that cabinet over there?" Big Jax glared at Josh and jerked his head to the large metal unit in the back of the room.

The vision of a large dragon roared into Josh's mind. Big Jax was muscular, a bit taller than Josh, three times his size, and Josh was on his own. But he was going to save Abby from this villain or die trying.

Eyes shifting, Josh moved toward the cabinet, never turning his back on Big Jax. He searched for something that could be used as a weapon.

As he reached the cabinet, Abby moaned, and he whipped his head up. "I said, 'Let her breathe, you moron. Or she won't be able to tell you anything.'"

"Where is the pain medicine?" Big Jax demanded, looking down at Abby.

Josh reached for the fire alarm above the cabinet, and a deafening clanging rang out.

The door burst open and the guard Tadd ran in and slid into Big Jax.

Tadd, Big Jax, and Abby fell onto the concrete floor of the infirmary.

The stench of sulfur filled the room. And in the dimming light a big cat emerged from the doorway.

The huge feline opened his mouth in an evil grin made more menacing by curved 20 inch long saber teeth extending from each side of his mouth. "You are at my mer-cee," he hissed.

Josh backed into the metal cabinet, his hands splayed against the drawers. Where were those warriors he'd seen when the dragon had pulled him from his cell.

Stretching his jaws wide, the big cat licked the sides of his mouth, slobbers dripping onto the floor. He rose on his back feet until he appeared as a mighty oak tree, and Josh bent his head backward to stare at the towering beast.

With no warning the beast's massive front paw slapped at Josh.

Josh jumped back, barely avoiding a blow to the head. "Help me, Jesus," he cried.

The animal screeched as if he had been stabbed.

In an instant, Josh felt cold steel against the palm of his hand. When he looked down, he clutched a glistening silver sword. Could it be?

"Call upon Me while I can be found," the Spirit whispered to him. "I am stronger than the demon Eligos."

"Yes, Lord," Josh murmured. Armor covered his chest. "Greater is He who is in me than the ruler of this evil world."

With a lunge, Josh buried his sword into the cat's belly.

"Not again," Eligos wailed as he withered away.

"When you put your trust in Me, I will fight your battles with you. Well done, warrior," the Spirit said.

Josh looked at the three who were out cold on the floor. Grabbing a roll of strong tape, he pulled Big Jax's arms behind his back and began wrapping his wrists together.

The words of Amazing Grace reverberated in his mind as he finished the make-shift bonds.

With a wad of gauze, he tickled the guard's nose, who sneezed and glanced at Abby.

More guards entered the room and, loaded Big

Jax on a gurney. Dark clouds covered them all as they wheeled him away.

~*~

Abby woke up in the Emergency Department of the hospital with a bandage on her throat. "What?"

And then the memory of Big Jax's attack hit her. "Hello?" she croaked.

A nurse entered the cubicle. "Hey, Abby. How are you feeling?" the pretty blonde with Mediterranean heritage greeted her.

"Hi, Erin." Abby's hand rose to her throat. "I've been better. But thanks for taking good care of me."

"I think you are very lucky, girlfriend."

"You know better than that. Luck had nothing to do with it," Abby replied. "It was God in action."

Erin nodded. "Someone upstairs likes you alright."

"How long have I been here?"

"About three hours. You opened your eyes once or twice but went out again."

Abby felt the back of her head. "I must have fallen on something really hard."

'Yep, but the scan was okay." Erin tilted her head and examined her friend. "How's your vision?"

"It's good."

"Okay. Great. Dr. Everett Hamilton will be in here in a few minutes and then maybe you can go home and rest."

"Wait. How did I get here?"

# Awareness

"Riding in the back of the ambulance with a handsome blonde man in a uniform," Erin teased with a twinkle in her eye.

"Really?" Abby laughed. "Last time I saw him, he was flat on his back on the floor."

Tadd slipped into the room. "That would be me, Ma'am."

Abby felt her cheeks burn. "You better quit sliding through doorways. The last time you did that you were knocked out cold."

"Well, then you better get out of this hospital so I can take you home," he retorted with a cocky grin. "By the way, your good friend, Janet brought my car to me."

"Janet?" Abby felt her spirits lift. "Is she here?"

"No, sorry. Guess I should have said Anthony and Janet shuttled my car over here. They've already left."

*Before I even got released? Things must still be in an uproar at the prison.* But Anthony was taking his State Boards, and Janet, no doubt, had to return to work. Made sense.

Once the doctor released Abby to return home, Tadd helped her go outside to his car.

She leaned her head back and enjoyed the ride. *"I could get used to this."*

~*~

Michael had heard all about the fight in the infirmary during meal time, and he found Josh waiting in the cell when he returned.

"Have you heard anything about Abby? I wanted so badly to go with her to the hospital."

"Yeah, I understand. Just like I felt helpless because I couldn't go back home with Deborah." Michael grabbed his Bible off the top bunk and slid down the wall to sit on the floor. "The fight was all the talk in the cafeteria. You must have fought an awesome fight in there."

"Well, like you said, it wasn't me, it was God. Boy, did I feel the Holy Spirit give me strength and courage. I've never felt like that before. He told me I was a warrior and that it was His battle."

Just then Janet came down the hall to their cell. "Don't worry, guys, I just heard from Abby. She's fine. The hospital patched her up and sent her home to rest."

"Thanks, Janet." Josh gave her a grateful look. "How did she get home? She didn't drive herself, did she?"

"No, one of our guards took her home."

"A guard? Who?"

"Tadd James, one of the guards from this section."

Was that good or bad? Josh glanced at Michael, but neither of them said a word.

"Josh," Janet whispered. "Welcome to the team."

~*~

Abby fixed a cup of coffee for Tadd and herself

and took it out to the deck. The air was cool, and the moon was big and bright as they sat outside enjoying the night sounds.

"Abby, I am so glad you weren't hurt today. That was a mighty brave thing the prisoner did in stopping Big Jax."

"He's not just a prisoner, Tadd. His name is Josh Pennington. And I will be forever grateful to him."

"Oh, sorry, I apologize. 'Haven't learned all the names yet. Did you know him before he arrived at the prison?"

"No. I—I. Well, let's just say, I knew of him from a friend," Abby was not going to delve into Josh's relationship with the team at this point. "He seems to be a good man."

"Well, something landed him in prison," Tadd replied carefully.

"That's right. Sometimes people make a wrong choice, and they let this world get the best of them for a while."

"Yes they do." Tadd looked at his hands and then at Abby "What's your favorite food?"

"If I'm going to a restaurant I love Italian and some Mexican dishes. But my absolute favorite food is some I was served in the Dominican when a work team from our church went down there. Why do you ask?"

He grinned. "I'm considered a pretty good cook so why don't I fix something for you tomorrow evening? I'll bring the ingredients and do the cooking if you help me do the eating."

"Now how could I say no to an opportunity like that?" she teased.

He put his coffee cup down. "Then it's a deal. Say about seven?"

"That's good. I'll look forward to it. Only I should be cooking for you, considering how good you've been to me."

"Oh, no. You just rest and feel better." He reached over and gently covered her hand with his. "I like you, Abby, and I enjoyed your company tonight." Then he got up, walked to the steps at the back of the deck and turned around to smile at her. "Bye."

She couldn't keep her eyes off him as he descended the steps to the driveway, got into his car, and drove away.

"Wow," she whispered to the stars, "He is definitely good-looking. God, are you thinking what I'm thinking?"

~*~

"Hey, sis. We have another team member." Anthony called out as Janet entered the apartment that evening.

"That's great. Now there are five of us."

"I wonder who will be next."

Janet's eyes twinkled. "Oh, God's got all of this planned out."

"Janet. What do you mean? Do you know

something more?"

"Could be. God's rarely silent, you know, little brother."

## CHAPTER 30

"I'm what?" Josh's eyes widened in amazement, "Did you just say I am getting out of prison? Why am I getting out early?"

"I said." Josh's attorney looked at him intently. "You are getting out of *this* prison, and being moved to a small town about an hour away."

"But why?" Josh asked.

"It's about the other prisoner, Big Jax. For some reason, he's got it in for you."

"You got that right."

"Of course, I do. That's my job. Anyway he's making death threats. And he is so huge they can hardly handle him."

"Yeah, chatter on the grapevine says he's almost seven feet tall and weighs in at over four hundred pounds."

"So you understand this move is for your own safety. Besides, you don't have much longer, and the prison you're going to is not that much different than this one. Maybe a bit less rigid, maybe more. Not sure who the current warden is, actually. But aren't you happy about the move?"

Josh sat across the table feeling perplexed. How would he get along in the new prison without

Michael? "I guess. When do I leave?"

"In the morning," The attorney answered, picking up his briefcase. "They are not taking any chances that Big Jax might come after you when they aren't around."

~*~

Josh was transported to a prison at Slattersville, Ohio by a woman deputy named Pat. He watched her through the bars which separated him from the front. She was a matter-of-fact type but with a pleasant enough attitude. However Josh could sense a toughness about her. Likely she could get nasty if she needed to.

He could feel her eyes on him as she glanced in her rear view mirror every now and then during the forty-five minutes of the drive. She made a few comments about the weather and traffic.

For his part, he planned to keep the ride as calm as possible, and kept his replies respectful. He sure didn't need to give her any cause to report him. He didn't want to risk more time being added to his sentence.

Hopefully this was the last time he would be moved before he was able to gain his freedom. But, the bad thing was, he was just getting used to the team and this warrior thing.

He already missed Michael back at the former prison. Stupid? Yes, probably. But their friendship meant a lot to him.

Michael was a man Josh knew he could trust. While most prisoners would as soon lie as they would breathe. Like Big Jax who was out to get him.

Josh trembled. If he thought about Big Jax too much, he would lose it. He fought to prevent fear taking hold of his mind. Big Jax was a mean, ferocious guy. He didn't care who he hurt—not even Abby.

But the memory of his own, pre-Jesus, callous actions rushed him. How he used to hurt others just to have drugs. He may not have tried to kill anyone, but he sure plotted to hurt anyone who got in his way over the junk out there on the streets. He closed his eyes as shame engulfed him.

"Remember, you are forgiven. The past has been washed away," God spoke gently but firmly to his heart. "Do not drag it back up."

Josh bowed his head. "Forgive me for shaming myself, Lord. You died for all my sins. Please take this fear away."

~*~

Back at Clanston State Prison, loneliness washed over Michael. He hadn't known Josh long, but their brief encounter had turned into a real friendship, and he missed that.

Was his mission here at the prison over? As he sat on the floor with his treasured Bible open on his lap, he felt a stirring in his heart.

"Get ready you still have more work to do and

more battles to fight in here."

Footsteps approached his cell. The guard stood by the door with Big Jax. His huge tatted arms seemed to flash like neon lights.

Michael's heart pounded with fear and horror. *I am not going to survive the night with his big guy here, Oh, Lord help me, please.*

"Michael, do not fear. When I am with you, who can be against you? Hold on to your faith. Have I ever failed you?"

*No, Lord, please forgive me and help me through the night.*

Big Jax stumbled to the lower bunk and seemed to fall into a deep sleep.

What if he had chosen the top bunk? How strong were these cots anyway?

~*~

Becky couldn't think of anything else during the days after Anthony left New York except his prayer for their lives. *"Who is this God he is praying to? I remember a friend of mine who always went to church and constantly wanted me to go with her. She talked about Jesus just like Janet does, but I just don't know."*

As she turned those memories over and over in her mind, Becky kept thinking about Anthony's proposal for her to move to Ohio.

*He has surely changed.* She wondered if starting fresh in another place would be the best thing for them. Maybe she should try to pray about it.

She sat down on the couch in the living room and bowed her head. She didn't close her eyes but picked lint off her slacks as she began, "God, I don't really know you. I feel really silly talking out loud in an empty room. But maybe you can help me decide about this."

Becky shook her head and her long tresses brushed against her face. *I will have to do better than that.* I'll find a Bible. I know there's one in here somewhere.

She went to the only cabinet in the living room and searched in the very back. Her hand touched a book way back in the corner. "I found it," She said aloud.

Her mama had given the Bible to her when she was a little girl. *Maybe I'll sit down and read this a bit, and maybe it will explain to me what has happened to Anthony.*

Just as Becky began to flip through the pages, Ben came inside from his play. "Hi, honey, are you hungry?"

"Nope," he answered, "What are you readin', Mom?"

"It's an old Bible that Grandma Sonerita gave me when I was a little girl. Come sit with me, and let's look at it together."

Ben bounced down on the couch beside her. "Wow. It's a big book."

# Awareness

"Yes, let's see what's inside." Becky turned the pages and found many old pictures, newspaper clippings about her family and some of herself as a child, falling out and sliding into her lap.

"Look, Ben."

He laughed with her at some of the old hairstyles and out-of-style clothing. When she'd flipped several pages, she came to a familiar verse in the Bible itself.

"For God so loved the world, that He gave his only begotten son, that whosoever believeth in Him, should not perish but have everlasting life. That's John 3:16 and people quote it a lot."

Becky sat quietly for a moment after she read the verse. "I wonder if this verse helped your dad believe in God the way he does."

"Do you think that's why Dad talks to God?" Ben glanced at her and continued bouncing.

"Probably." She placed her hand on his shoulder. "Quit jumping on the couch. You sure have a lot of energy. Why don't we go for a walk?"

"Yay." Ben jumped to his feet, "Come on."

He was out the door before she could pick up her bag and a sweater. By the time she caught up with her son, they were approaching the park.

Ben pointed to the balloons and children with paint on their faces. "Look, Mom. Something fun is going on over there." He tried to pull away from her hand.

"Wait, Ben. We will be there in a minute. Slow down."

"Aw, Mom." He sighed but obeyed.

There was a tent with tables and what looked to be paint sets on them. An auburn haired man, twentyish, medium height, stood next to the entrance. He looked friendly enough in spite of his acne scarred complexion.

"Hi, folks, I'm Chris Parker, and we are doing free face-painting. Ma'am, would you let your son get his face painted?" he asked politely.

"Mom." Ben pleaded, "Please? Please?"

Becky held up her hand for him to stop begging.

"Are you sure it's free, Chris?"

"Yes, ma'am, all we need is your permission for your son to participate."

"I'm Ben," he shouted.

Chris grinned. "Yes. We need your permission to let Ben listen to a story about Jesus."

Becky looked at Ben. Was he interested?

He was still mouthing "Please?"

Her heart softened. She nodded that it was okay.

As Chris seated Ben, he also pulled up a chair for Becky. "Have a seat, ma'am. We love to have parents listen in."

Becky watched as Chris helped Ben choose a group of colorful balloons.

"Please stay real still, Ben, and listen to this very special story as I paint your face. It's important to be steady so your design will be just perfect."

"Okay." Ben sat quietly and watched the man.

"I'm going to lean close to your ear so I can tell the story and paint at the same time."

Becky was mesmerized for the next few minutes while this young man told the story of how Jesus came from Heaven—a Holy place without sin—to this sin-filled earth, because of God's plan to rescue people from being forever separated from Him.

"God loves us and wants us to live with Him forever," Chris explained.

She listened intently as Chris continued telling how it was God's plan for His Son, Jesus, to die on the cross and pay the price for sin so all people could be forgiven. How Jesus was put on the cross by evil men who plotted to kill Him. And although Jesus died, He didn't stay dead.

"On the third day, Jesus rose from the dead. He now lives in Heaven talking to God about us," Chris said. "And if we asked for forgiveness for the things we'd done wrong and believe that Jesus died for us, we can be with Him in Heaven one day. Not only that, but He would give us the power to live on this earth until then and help others come to accept Him."

When Chris was done with the story, He had painted four different colored balloons on Ben's face, each one representing a part of the story.

"Would you like to pray with me now to accept

Jesus into your heart Ben? It's easy, and I can help you."

Ben nodded,

When Chris glanced at Becky to see if it was acceptable to her, she couldn't prevent the tears slipping down her face.

"We would both like to accept Him, Chris," she whispered.

"Great. Just talk to God as if he is your very best friend. Because, He is."

"Jesus, I am sorry for the wrong things I have done. I'm sorry for not listening to Mom and Dad. Please forgive me and help me to do better. I believe you died for me. Amen. "

"Amen," Becky said as Ben finished his prayer. "Dear Jesus, I am so glad to meet you and to talk to you. I never knew how to, and I really messed up when I tried this at home a while ago. Now I think I will do it every day." She giggled nervously. "Forgive me for my sins. Jesus, I believe you died on the cross for me. Amen."

Then Chris prayed for both of them and thanked God for His mercy and kindness toward all believers.

At the final "Amen," Becky looked up at him. Chris was shedding a tear also. Seeing him in a new light, his scars appeared less noticeable.

She stood up to leave, but Ben ran to the painter and threw his arms around him.

# Awareness

"Mr. Chris, will you come to our house?"

"I can't come today but we'll be back here tomorrow. We're having hot dogs and ice cream. So why don't you and your mama come back then, and I'll walk you back home when we're done, if it's okay with her."

"Hot dogs and ice cream." Ben jumped up and down. "Mom, can we?"

She nodded. Her son never seemed to run out of energy.

"I'm not going to wash my face tonight. I want the balloons to be there tomorrow."

Chris waved as they walked away. "Okay. See you then."

"Wow, Mom," Ben said, "Wasn't that a grand surprise?"

She squeezed her son's hand. What would the boy say next? Her heart warmed at the thought of what she and her son had just done. She had never felt so happy or so free.

When they got home it was she who called Anthony. "Hello, Honey. You will never guess what happened today. Ben and I. We. The two of us. We asked Jesus into our hearts."

There was total silence on the other end of the phone.

"Honey? Honey?" she called to him.

"Hey, Dad, are you there? I have balloons on my face," Ben yelled toward the phone.

"What? When? How?"

Becky heard the astonishment and happiness in Anthony's voice. For once in her life, the happiness bubbling up inside of her almost prevented her from finishing the story of her and Ben's wonderful day.

## CHAPTER 31

The first rays of early morning light announced the long night was over.

Michael's cellmate continued snoring, which should have reassured him, but an overpowering sulfur smell filled the room, and darkness descended again.

"Time for battle, but do not fear, I will stand by you."

Even without much light, Michael recognized the armor coating his body, and the glimmer of swords revealed the heavenly army standing and ready for battle as well.

Just in time.

The massive legs and feet of the gargantuan dragon filled the small cell, leaving little space for movement.

From a human perspective, Botis, huge and terrible to look upon, seemed invincible.

But God had assured him that He was still near.

Yet, when Michael struck out with his blade, the dragon knocked it away as if it was a mere toy.

With his claw, the dragon grabbed Michael. In that instant the talons penetrated his armor and skin. Sticky liquid dripped down his back.

The dragon twisted his huge head toward Michael, his massive mouth opened, and with a roar the reptile spewed fire.

The intense heat laughed at Michael, and the flames licked blisters onto his body. He knew if help wasn't swift in coming, he'd be burnt to a crisp in minutes. "Lord, save me," he screamed.

Abby and Janet appeared at the cell door ready for battle as the huge creature leaned over Michael where he lay on the floor.

But when Janet swung her sword, it bounced off the dragon's tough hide, and he roared his displeasure.

Abby had slipped to the other side and swung her sword simultaneously with Janet. It swished on the empty air.

*What is happening? Has God forsaken us?* "Please God, we need you," Michael yelled.

"Stand up and fight," God said.

Strength and power rushed through Michael's body. He stood, picked up his sword, and sliced into one of the dragon's legs.

Janet aimed her sword at the tail.

Abby stepped forward and swung at the dragon's head. She missed.

Botis spit fire again. "This is my world and you cannot defeat me, weakling human beings that you are."

"We are weak but He is strong." Abby swung her

sword again and this time she stabbed the massive reptile in the eye.

The dragon roared.

"The blood of the Lamb will overcome you." Janet held up her sword.

"We fight in the almighty name of Jesus." Michael's sword clicked together with Janet's and merged into a huge silver javelin.

"This is now team fighting. Both of you grab the javelin and stab Botis in the heart," God said.

In total obedience, Michael and Janet both clasped hold onto the weapon and rammed it straight into the heart of the dragon.

The cell was filled with an unspeakable roar, and immediately, the darkness lifted.

The dragon was gone.

Only a smell of sulfur still lingered in the air, and Big Jax lay unconscious on the floor, bleeding and in great agony.

Once again guards transported Big Jax to the infirmary.

~*~

Chris sat at the kitchen table with Becky and her son Ben.

He had been a Christian since he was a kid in school, and now he was enjoying these two new believers as they related their conversation with Anthony the night before.

Their laughter touched his heart as they

recounted their attempts to fill Anthony in on their news.

Ben giggled as he said that all he could talk to his dad about was the balloons Chris had painted on his face.

Becky chuckled. "I was laughing so hard at this little man's antics I could hardly get any words out to explain all that had transpired."

Ben continued, "And when Dad asked, 'Who's Chris?' Mom and I just laughed more."

"Anthony probably thought we went crazy," Becky said with a smile. "I don't know when I've laughed so much."

"I believe God has given both of you the spirit of laughter. God is so awesome and He gives those who trust in Him many good things."

"Yes He does."

"By the way, where is your husband? Anthony, I believe you called him?"

"He is out of town. On a mission, you might say, in Ohio."

"Daddy talks to God," Ben added. "And God tells him what to do—he's on a team, you know."

"What kind of team?" Chris frowned as he tried to take it in.

Becky leaned back in her chair. "Anthony felt a call from God to go to others who needed hope in their lives, and fight for them. From what I can understand it's in a spiritual realm. I'm afraid I haven't been too supportive. In fact, until now I have been very opposed to him going off on these trips."

"Well, it's always hard when someone you care about is away serving the Lord. It's a struggle between what you feel is best and what the other person has been called by God to do." Chris nodded his understanding. "His ways are truly higher than our ways, and I had a hard time leaving my family—my Mom—and coming to New York to serve in this Child Evangelism Program."

"How long will you be on this mission?"

"I don't know. Whatever God says. I never know when or where He will send me next." Chris paused and sipped his drink.

"It was hard for both of us when I got the call, because Mom is sickly, and I was her only family close by."

"These are hard decisions." Becky's words were low and sympathetic.

"Yes, for some more than others." Chris sighed. "Now tell me about this team."

They spent the next hour talking about what Becky knew—which wasn't a lot.

Ben added to the discussion in his own exuberant way. And they laughed and talked until late afternoon.

"I would love to know more about this mission of your husband's. It sounds so interesting and exciting."

"Well, I've been thinking about making a trip to see them, so if you'd like to come along with us, you may," Becky said.

"Yeah, Mr. Chris, please?"

"Now, Ben, don't try to persuade Mr. Parker."

"Oh, nobody will have to persuade me, Mrs. Becky." Chris reached over and tussled Ben's short brown hair. "I would love to go."

"Anthony says it's a ten hour drive. So we will stay with some of the team while we are there. How about leaving Monday morning around 9:00? Are you staying close by? We can pick you up."

"I'm just down the street at the church that sponsored the Fun Day at the park. I'll be there by 9 am, all packed and ready to help you drive."

"Yay." Ben exuberantly proceeded to dance around the kitchen.

~*~

Abby and Janet were lounging in the living room of Deborah's house when Anthony entered.

He glanced at the two women with concern in his eyes. "I feel like I've been neglecting you girls. I've had my nose in the books while I studied for the State Exams. It's just—I need to continue to practice law in Ohio. Now it's all over but the waiting."

Janet patted his shoulder. "We understand. Don't we, Abby?"

She did understand in a way. But wasn't he supposed to be their leader? And while he'd been tied up they had to make their own decisions. Well. They probably should always make their own decisions. Abby waited to see what Anthony would have to say.

"Now that I have come up for air, why don't you tell me what's going on in your lives?"

"I've been seeing someone." Abby brushed her hair out of her face. She'd left it down. No pony tail today. "Not in a serious way, although it could develop into that. He's not a Christian yet but shows signs of interest. So for now, he's just a friend."

"Is he interested in a relationship with the Lord or with you?"

Abby looked at him intently. He was not teasing. His face was serious.

"Possibly both," she replied cautiously, not sure she was comfortable with where Anthony was going with this question.

"Anyone I know?" Anthony asked.

"I'm not sure. His name is Tadd, and he's a guard at the prison. He's got a background in military operations, and he thinks he may be moving to a little town called Slattersville, to work.

"Be careful, Abby," Anthony warned. "Look." He covered her hand with his. "I'm not trying to be mean or anything, but I can't help but worry about you."

"I'm good, Anthony," she replied with a bit of a bite. "I can take care of myself. Really. I've taken care of myself for a long time now."

"Well, I am concerned about you personally." Anthony looked at Janet and back to Abby. "But, if I can come clean with both of you, I'm concerned about the team more than our individual lives at the moment."

"What are you talking about, little brother? The team is growing. Instead of the three of us, like at the beginning, there are now five."

"It's not the numbers, sis. It's our strength, or lack thereof."

"And what's wrong with our strength?" Abby challenged. "We have fought Satan's forces since we banded together and won every single one."

"Did we?"

Abby looked from Anthony to Janet. Janet didn't seem to understand his words any better than she did.

"You see," Anthony continued. "That's where we are weak. It's not about us, it's about the Lord, and I'm not sure we are where we need to be. This team has to be dependent upon the Lord. These battles are His. Not ours."

Abby sat quietly, with downcast eyes.

"Brother, you are right," Janet said. "I haven't devoted as much of my personal time in prayer like, at least, like I did when I first came here. My emotions have pulled me down somewhat. And I have been feeling, I don't know, lonely maybe. We haven't attended church other than the one time I went with Abby. We need the gathering of ourselves together with other believers. At least I—for one need it."

"We all do." Abby rallied. "Here's a suggestion for you. Tomorrow is Sunday. Why don't we all attend my church? Let's invite Deborah to come as well. She shouldn't stay home just because Michael can't go." Abby looked forward to more of the team visiting New Hope Trinity church.

The three of them agreed to be ready the next morning, and Janet said she would tell Deborah their plans.

"Now, we need to discuss some personal business," Anthony continued. "Becky and Ben will be here Monday evening. Their new friend Chris Parker is coming along with them. He will need a place to stay."

"We can't suggest the guest room in Deborah's house since Michael isn't home." Janet pursed her lips and then made her decision. "I better give up my room in the cottage."

"And then I'll need to talk to Becky about moving so we'll need some private time. We might need a babysitter, even though Ben's not exactly a baby."

"No problem there. I'll take the job," Janet said. "I can't wait to see my nephew."

"Thanks, sis. And I want Chris to meet the team."

"And I want to meet your family," Abby said with

a nod.

"After church tomorrow, I'd like to stop by the prison to see Michael. I know how much he misses Deborah and the rest of us, as well as Josh, since he's been moved to—" He broke off and looked at Abby, "Hey, didn't you say the guy you were seeing, this guy Tadd? Didn't you say he might be moving to work at a town called Slattersville?"

"Uh, yeah. That was the town he mentioned. Why do you ask?"

"Did you know that's where they've moved Josh?"

"That's right, his transfer papers said, Slattersville, Ohio. I remember from when I was typing them up last week." Janet's eyes widened. "A coincidence?"

Anthony looked at Abby. "You sure it was Slattersville?"

"Absolutely," Abby said. "What are you thinking?"

"I know it's not a coincidence," Anthony stated confidently. "Has anything that has happened to us lately been a coincidence? "

"No," they all said in unison.

Could it be? Was God about to show His power again? And in another place?

## CHAPTER 32

God blessed Abby with a stunning sunset, on her way home from the team meeting. By the time she reached her house the street lights had come on.

As she turned into her drive, Abby noticed someone standing on her front porch. She didn't see a car parked anywhere. In the twilight she couldn't see well enough to recognize who it was, but as she swung her car lights in that direction, she realized it was Tadd.

She grinned to herself and unbuckled her seatbelt. Then with her hand on the unlock button, she hesitated. *What is Tadd doing here, showing up on my porch without calling? How did he get here?*

Suddenly he was at her window and she gasped. *I should have picked up Grizzly from the vet today.* She shook her head. *What is wrong with me? Tadd is a friend, and here I sit like a scared kid.*

Abby let her window down. "What on earth are you doing here this time of the night?"

"Did I frighten you? I am so sorry, Abby. I apologize," he said earnestly. "I thought you'd recognize me."

"But what are you doing here?"

"I was out on a run and just decided to check on

you. A spur-of-the-moment thing. Didn't realize you weren't home."

"I don't know what's wrong with me. I guess I'm just jumpy tonight." As Abby exited the car she felt his arms go around her, and he pulled her tightly to him. Before she could back-up, he was kissing her face and neck.

"Tadd. Stop." She panicked and pushed her arms against him. Although they were close in height she knew he could easily overpower her.

At her resistance he stepped back and she could breathe easier.

"I'm sorry Abby. You just looked so gorgeous in the moonlight, and you smell so good. I'm so sorry." His arms were now at his side and his face downcast.

"I'm not ready for that kind of a relationship. We just met. You have to understand I don't know you that well."

"You don't have to explain a thing. I must be going. Please forgive me. I can't say how sorry I am." He turned hurriedly and started back on his run up the street.

She looked toward her garage and took a deep breath. *I left the stupid door open again.*

Then another thought startled her. *He had known I wasn't here. He had to have seen my car wasn't in the garage. But still, he just waited for me to come home. "*

~*~

# Awareness

Anthony mulled over the latest meeting of the team. He was still concerned about Abby. She had been upset when he briefly mentioned she should be careful. He was uneasy about that. The words that came into his mind were *rebellious spirit.*

And then there was his sister, Janet. She was getting touchy too, seemed a bit lonely and distracted. Maybe going to church tomorrow together would be a good thing, especially for her.

Another concern for Michael and Deborah was that they were having separation issues.

And Josh. Anthony shook his head in disappointment. In this new prison, Josh seemed more afraid than he had been in the actual battle with Big Jax. What was all that about?

Until just lately, the team had been strengthened, after battles.

And now Becky and Ben would be here Monday. Even though they had accepted Jesus, would his wife be any more eager to leave New York and join him?

Then he realized he would have to find a job—perhaps start that business—to support the family. There would be the chore of getting a place to stay as well. Well, not a chore. Never a chore.

And what about Chris? Would he be one of them? Was God calling him to the team effort?

"Stress," Anthony muttered, rubbing his hands over his face. He felt drained and tired. For the first in a very long time, he longed for a drink.

"Lord," he asked, "What is happening to us? To Your team?"

~*~

Still shaking from the encounter with Tadd, Abby realized her angst was mostly from knowing he'd lied to her. She questioned herself over and over again about the incident and about her reaction to it.

She needed to talk to someone and phoned Erin. There was no answer so she left a message.

*Am I just being silly? His background is not the same as mine. He is not a Christian. Am I being ridiculous over nothing?*

Her cell rang and showed Erin's ID.

"Hello?" Abby answered.

"Hi, friend. What's happening?" Erin came back with her usual bubbly reply.

"I need some advice."

"Sounds serious."

"Kind of," Abby replied. "Can you come over? Like right now?"

"Sure. Seen *handsome* lately?" Erin inquired.

"We'll talk when you get here." Abby ended the call.

~*~

"Well, I guess that answers my question." Erin grabbed her keys and headed out the door.

When she arrived at Abby's place, she found her

friend sitting on the front steps in the moonlight, and looked at her intently. "Hey, Abby, are you okay? "

Abby burst into tears. Erin sat down and put her arm around her. "What's wrong, sweetie? "

Abby shook her head so Erin just sat beside her and waited like a good friend.

When she calmed, Abby explained what had happened. "I just don't understand, Erin. Why would he lie to me? I thought he cared about me."

"Maybe he cares too much," Erin said quietly.

Abby turned to look into her face. "What do you mean he cares too much?"

"Well, maybe he has issues with getting too close to ladies, too fast." Erin hugged her knees. "You know some guys just don't have a good understanding about what makes a woman like you tick. They think they can jump from a nice dinner to a roll in the hay."

Abby chuckled. "Not this gal."

"He's probably as confused as you are."

"Maybe. But waiting for me here without calling. It scared me. And then he lied to me about it."

"Then just tell him that. Remember, he is not a Christian. He may not understand boundaries so you need to set them, and back them up if he gets pushy."

Abby sighed. "You make me feel so much better. You are a good friend, Erin."

"That's me," she teased. "Remember, God knows how you feel, just talk to Him about it."

"I will." Abby gave Erin a hug. "Why didn't I stop to pray before I opened the car door?"

## CHAPTER 33

Janet wanted to drive her Honda Civic to church that morning. Said she knew the way. So Anthony graciously waved Deborah into the front passenger seat, and then conceded to sit in the back of the car.

He probably ought to swallow his pride and sell the Porsche. What would Becky have to say about that?

When they reached the church, Anthony eyed the old brick building. He found it impressive. It had several arched type double doors. Janet naturally walked toward the set under the bell tower since the church sign was attached just to the right of the doors. He smirked. It was so Janet to hone in on the correct set of doors.

When they entered the sanctuary his eyes were drawn to the story told panel by panel by the stained glass mosaics in the arched windows. The sun shone through the high round window above them, throwing a rainbow of colored light over the pews.

Janet tugged lightly on his arm and he followed his sister and Deborah as they moved forward to sit with Abby and her friend Erin.

When they reached the pew, Abby reached over and welcomed each of them with a smile, and "God

Bless you."

The organist began the prelude, and they all quickly took their places. Soon the varied voices of the choir floated from the loft blessing all in the sanctuary.

Anthony glanced at his sister and smirked at the way her fingers danced across her lap as though she were playing one of the instruments.

When the music finished, and the choir was seated, a middle-aged gentleman stepped to the podium.

"Welcome everyone, members and visitors alike. My name is Reverend Robert Milton, and I want to thank you for coming to worship with us this morning."

The congregation clapped politely, and the reverend humbly bowed his head. Then he looked over the sanctuary. "And thank you to this congregation for allowing me to serve you in the face of my father's declining health."

The reverend's voice was strong and steady enough to hold Anthony's attention. "We will open with a prayer, and then I've asked the choir to immediately sing the hymn which holds the same title as the sermon I want to deliver today. *There Is Power In The Blood.* Please bow your heads."

After the service Reverend Milton greeted each one at the door as they left. When Janet reached him, he took her hand in his. "Who do you have with you today?"

She looked up into his face and seemed to have lost her voice.

Anthony stepped up and grasped the minister's hand. "Great message, sir. I'm Janet's brother, Anthony Markson, and this is our friend Deborah Reeves."

"Glad to have you with us," the reverend said. Then he glanced at Abby, "You just might win the prize for bringing the most guests this month."

~*~

With a song in her heart, Janet drove to Abby's favorite café for dinner.

"Well, how did you like the service?" Abby asked after they were seated.

"The *Power in the Blood* message was just what we needed this morning," Anthony said. "I mentioned that I appreciated it to the reverend."

Janet grinned. "I know I told you this the last time, but the church really is gorgeous. I felt satisfied just sitting there and absorbing the atmosphere."

Anthony glanced at Deborah. "Do you think you could feel at home in this church? We want to find a place where we are all comfortable."

She shrugged. "Well, you know I miss Michael. So until he can give his input, I'll just let the rest of you lead the way. Who knows how long it will be before he can join us?"

Abby put her arm around Deborah. "I'll do my best to make you feel welcome. I'll try to introduce you to some women your age the next time you come."

Janet's eyes widened. "Didn't know age was so important. Maybe you need to introduce me to the middle aged crowd too."

~*~

That afternoon Janet sat in the kitchen, flipping through a cooking magazine, her mind on the sermon this morning, and to be honest, she couldn't get her mind off the minister's spellbinding blue eyes. Why had she stood there like a shy child when he'd questioned her after church?

The phone rang, and it took a moment for her to drag herself back from the image of the handsome reverend before she reached for it and identified herself.

"Ms. Janet, this is Robert Milton. I hope I'm not calling you in the middle of something, but I wanted to ask you if I could take you somewhere for dinner this evening before church, say at five?"

"Tonight? Sure, Reverend." Was that her voice, calm and matter-of-fact when astonishment and pleasure were the primary emotions raging inside her?

"Please call me Robert," he said. "Can I pick you up?"

"Oh, no, why don't I meet you at the church, and

we can go from there, if that's okay?"

"Perfect. See you then."

When she ended the call, she sat down on the bed and took a deep breath. "What was all that about?"

Robert Milton arrived at exactly five o'clock, and she got in his car to ride to a nearby restaurant. "How do you like our town of Clanston?"

"It's very nice. I haven't been here long enough to see much of it."

"Do you work somewhere?"

"Yes, I'm an administrative assistant at the local prison."

"Really?" His brows rose. "Do you like working there?"

"It's okay. I taught school last year but when my brother came here to help someone, I decided to check the place out as well." Janet avoided the rest of the story. She wasn't ready to answer questions about the team right now.

"Well, I have assumed the position of pastor at my father's church. He's getting older and not in good health. He's just not able to manage things as he once did—especially the church's finances. I was an accountant so I was able to step in and help." Pride bled through his words, but Janet couldn't see as it hurt the facts of his statements.

After all, she was basking in his admiring looks and generous compliments. She was overwhelmed with his abilities and was seeing herself quite differently than she had in the past.

That night when Robert led her to his father and introduced her, Janet eyed the elderly minister. He was such a kind and humble man, yet she sensed despair in him as he interacted with the congregation. In fact he seemed to have aged from earlier in the day.

What on earth was going on?

## CHAPTER 34

That afternoon Deborah sat across from Michael in the visitation area of the prison. He looked depressed, and she knew for a fact that she was. "Honey, are you alright?"

"I guess as alright as you can be in a place like this."

She was sure she heard a streak of anger in his answer.

"I miss Josh," he continued. "I don't get to see you except on weekends, and I can't even touch you for this glass." He banged his hand against the window with a dull thud, and the guard standing near the door glanced his way.

"Honey, you will be okay. I understand. It's hard for me too." A tear slid down her cheek. "Are you able to study your Bible?"

"Of course. But I miss Josh. And so much has happened." He looked into her eyes. "I'm sorry for being such a grump. I just hate where I am. Why did God give me a new heart and then put me in this stinking place away from you?"

"Michael, God did not put you in there," she reminded him. "But He can use you while you're here."

He stiffened. "Don't preach to me."

"Michael, don't you talk to me like that. I'm not going back to where we were before."

"Sorry." Anger burned on his face as he stood. "I just can't talk right now."

He called the guard and walked away from her without looking back.

She sat crying silently for a while, and shook her head. She did not want this kind of life. "Lord, help me."

~*~

When she got home that evening Deborah telephoned the hospital for the name of a psychologist near Clanston. She was given the name of Dr. Sandra Beazel along with her phone number.

She determined to call in the morning to make an appointment. Something was wrong, and perhaps this woman could help.

Deborah remembered her life prior to Anthony coming to visit them and helping Michael overcome his demons. She was not willing to go back to the old life. It had been a miserable and scary time for her, and she could not bear any more abuse.

~*~

Abby had invited Tadd over to talk. Erin was right. Confronting him would give her a chance to set her boundaries.

He said he would be able to come about 7:00 o'clock, and she agreed, even though it meant she had to miss the evening church service.

Abby dressed casually in jeans and a top. And since she didn't' want to appear to be enticing him, she ignored her favorite perfume.

When she opened the door at his knock, he was also dressed casually in jeans and a T-shirt. Handsome, as usual, he seemed uneasy but she smiled and welcomed him in as though they were still good friends. Which they probably were.

"Come in, Tadd. Good to see you. Let's sit in the living room." She gestured him inside. No more stars and moonlight tonight.

"Sure, thanks."

"Tadd, I just wanted to talk with you about the other night."

"Listen, Abby, I am so sorry"

"Wait, let me finish. I want to say how sorry I am that I allowed that to happen. I was not being careful. And I have to admit I have a problem knowing you lied to me."

"Yes, I did." His eyes glanced away from hers as he spoke. "I apologize for that. I knew you weren't home as soon as I noticed your car was not here."

"Thank you for admitting that. I realized it as soon as I saw I'd left the garage door open. "Now I want to talk about boundaries."

This time he didn't interrupt.

"I am a Christian, and you know that already. I know some people say they are Christians but live however they like. But I'm not like that. I live with boundaries because I know that's what God wants me to do."

She looked straight at him willing him to look back. "Do you understand what I'm saying?"

"Sure, Abby." He looked up at her with a pained expression.

"Now I'm not perfect by any stretch of the imagination but I try to live as close as possible to what God wants for my life. That's why I limit myself to what I will and will not do, and that includes getting too intimate with anyone."

Tadd shifted in his chair. "I don't want to be like that either. I struggle desperately with it. I always have. It bothers me constantly, and I can't seem to control it."

Her eye caught something just beyond him. She gasped. A gigantic moth had covered the entire wall in the living room. The creature's eyes were brilliant and the large mouth appeared capable of chewing almost anything of any size. Teeth clamped shut, it glared at her. Its giant, dull-brown wings stretched from ceiling to floor. Written over the wings was the word LUST.

*A demon.*

"Fear not, I will fight the battle for you," God spoke to her aloud. "Stand your ground."

Rising from the end of the couch she was immediately clothed in armor and sword.

Tadd, still seated, looked up at her. "Abby, are you all right? Who is talking to you?"

"God is talking to me, and I am okay. But please stay seated. I have to do battle for you."

"Me? Battle what?" He started to stand.

"No. Stay seated. I need the space. I'll explain later."

With that she felt her helmet rest on her shoulders. She extended her sword as she moved around the couch and behind him.

"In the name of Jesus Christ, be gone." Abby swung her sword again and again until she had sliced the giant moth into many pieces.

"Let me pray for you, Tadd."

She quietly put her hand on his shoulder. "Father God, you have been here tonight, and you have taken care of the battle against Satan once more. May Tadd be forever loosed from this demon of lust. In your Holy Name, Amen."

Tadd glanced at her, visibly confused and shaken. "What is going on, Abby? What just happened?"

She sat down beside him. "I am a member of an elite team of warriors for the Lord. There are things we can see and hear that come straight from God. He opens our eyes to the tactics Satan uses to come against us and others around us."

"Wow."

"We are only able to fight against them through the power which God has given us. I just fought a demon for you. We can't fight and win these battles on our own until we give ourselves over to God. That's why you are struggling."

Tadd stared at the floor and then he turned to look into her eyes. "I know you wouldn't lie to me, but you'll have to admit, that's some story."

She shrugged. "Yes, however, it's a true story. A demon appeared here represented as a huge moth which would have covered and taken control over you. The word LUST was engraved upon its wings in large block letters."

"Ewwe."

"Yeah. This demon, Asmodee, has probably been covering and smothering you all your life. From what you have told me about your struggles, it's been there a while."

Tadd dropped his head and stared at his hands. "Since I was a teen. I'm embarrassed to say this to you, but I was into porn really deep." He looked back at her with widened eyes. "You fought that?"

"Yes I did, but all I had to do was have faith. It was God's battle."

"I want faith like yours, Abby."

His words rang out, and she knew he was sincere.

"Then you must ask for it. You have to give yourself over entirely to God, and the way you do that is to admit your wrongs and ask forgiveness because of what Jesus did for all of us on the cross. He took our sins and gives us his righteousness."

"But that seems too simple."

Abby grinned. "It is. But once you do it, you must continue to follow Him. The exciting thing is, as you do, He gives you more faith."

"Really?"

"Absolutely. The power comes when you surrender your life and pledge to serve him." She looked at Tadd. "Are you ready to make the first step?"

"I am," he admitted. "Will you help me?"

"Of course, I will."

She reached for his hand and Tadd began to pray.

## CHAPTER 35

Josh claimed the lower bunk in his new cell. He opened his skimpy bag of belongings and pulled out his Bible. He'd just placed it on the bed beside him when a guard appeared with another prisoner.

With a clank, a jerk, and the squeal of metal in need of lubrication, the door to the cell was unlocked.

The guard shoved the prisoner inside. "Here's your new home."

He glanced at Josh and continued. "Enjoy your new roommate." He smirked and nodded as the door locked behind the new prisoner. "Make yourselves comfortable."

Skinny and tall, about the same height as Josh's own six and a half feet, the newcomer drug one foot as he moved toward the bunks. His black hair was sprinkled with gray, and his weathered face etched with an expression of deep sadness.

"Here, you can take the lower bunk." Josh stood and picked up his Bible.

The older man didn't say a word or even look at Josh. He simply continued toward the lower bunk, threw his small bag of belongings underneath, and fell onto the bunk. With awkward grace, he lifted his feet from the floor, rolled over, and curled up in a near fetal position.

Josh shrugged and laid his Bible on the top bunk. But as soon as he released it, a lonely feeling engulfed him, filling him with despair until he felt his emotions dragging the floor.

He looked around for a place to stash his own stuff, but his cellmate made him feel so uncomfortable he decided to keep it on the top bunk and use it for a pillow.

He picked up his Bible and he slid to the floor. He missed Clanston prison and his old cellmate Michael.

When the dinner alarm rang, the guard's feet tramped down the hall. But Josh's cellmate still hadn't said a word or moved a muscle since he'd entered the cell.

Was the ashen faced man still alive?

But as one of the guards stopped beside their cell door and called "Line up," the man managed to slowly turn and sit up on his bunk. Then, as if he had done it a million times, the old man stood, stepped to the door, and filed out into the line forming in the hall.

Josh quickly stepped in behind him.

The line moved to the dining hall where each man picked up a plate and moved along the food line.

Unrecognizable lumps of food spat onto the

trays.

Josh, of course, was beside his cellmate. No talking was the rule in this place. The silent line of men in grey jail clothes advanced to the tables and stopped in front of the place where each one would sit.

Another bell sounded, and every man sat down. The clank of metal eating utensils on metal plates filled the room, but Josh could hear whispering here and there.

Like the other prisoners Josh kept his head low, then he leaned toward his cellmate. "What's your name?" he whispered.

"Viper." His cellmate said no more as he continued to shovel the food into his mouth.

~*~

That evening the team gathered for a specially called meeting in Deborah and Michael's living room.

Janet had gone over earlier to help, and to move her things to the main house, allowing the expected visitor to use her room in the guest house while he was here.

Other than her, Anthony arrived first for the meeting.

"Good evening, brother." Janet gave him a hug. "You were up early this morning. I didn't even hear you leave for your run."

"That's because you were snoring so hard," he

teased. "Tired from your late night date, I expect."

She made a face at him. "I was not on a hot date. For your information, I was at church last night."

The door opened and Abby came in. A man about her height trailed behind her. "Tadd wanted to meet all of you. He is a new believer who just put his faith in Jesus last evening."

"Welcome, Tadd." Janet clapped her hands. "The more the merrier.

Anthony wiggled his eyebrows at Abby, and then turned to Tadd. "My name is Anthony, and I've heard a few things about you."

"Uh oh. I'm in trouble, and I just got here." Tadd rubbed his hand across his blonde hair.

At that moment, there was a light knock on the door, but before Janet could get up to open it, Ben burst inside.

"Aunt Janet." He grabbed her and nearly knocked her over.

She wrapped her arms around her nephew and picked him up.

"Janet, he's too heavy for you," Becky said as she and another man came in the door.

"You have grown," Janet ignored her sister-in-law's chiding, but let Ben slide out of her arms to the floor.

Then turning to Becky, Janet gave her a hearty hug. "I've missed both of you so."

"Dad," Ben shouted as he wrapped his arms about

his dad. "I've missed you."

"I've missed you too, son." Anthony leaned down and hugged Ben tightly. "But you don't have to yell."

"Now let me say hello to your mom." Anthony straightened and looked at Becky as he moved toward her. "Hi, honey. So glad you all made it safely." He leaned over and gave her a kiss.

Janet enjoyed watching her tall blonde brother and his shorter Latino wife. Whew, her brother's prolonged greeting to his wife made Janet want to giggle.

Finally he turned to the man who had entered the house with his family. "I'm so glad to meet you. Chris? Is that right?"

"Glad to meet you too." Chris held out his hand.

"Welcome to Clanston. I'm so grateful for what you've done for my family. Thanks for coming with Becky and Ben."

"I was just doing what God told me to do."

Deborah entered the room dressed in long shorts, T-shirt, and a broad-brimmed hat. "Glad you all made it here safely. Welcome to our home, my friends. Make yourselves comfortable."

She moved her gaze to the strangers. "You must be Ben and Becky. I was just getting ready to take advantage of the last bit of light we have left to work outside in the garden. You two are welcome to join me while our team has their meeting."

"Oh, boy, can we, Mom?" Ben asked. "Please?"

Becky ruffled her son's hair. "Stop with the begging, son. As long as we won't get in Mrs. Deborah's way, it will be fine."

"I would love for you to join me. We can talk and get to know each other," Deborah said. "Don't worry. I'll put this boy to work."

She handed him the basket filled with small garden tools.

"Yay." Ben skipped as he followed Deborah out of the room.

After another lingering kiss with Anthony, Becky trailed after her son toward the kitchen and back door.

This time Janet did giggle. "Missing her pretty badly huh?"

Her brother ignored her.

"Do you mind if I sit in on the meeting?" Chris asked

~*~

"Not at all." Anthony clapped the younger man on the shoulder. "We were expecting you to join us, and we have another guest as well."

As he introduced Chris and Tadd, Anthony pulled up some extra chairs and moments later they all found seats around the table.

For a moment, the group sat silently while Anthony looked at each of them with a grateful heart. These were God's people whom He had brought together. They had come so far and yet still had a long way to go.

Chris and Tadd had not yet fought their first battle. But if God decided to call them, He would see them through.

Abby and Janet had both fought battles on their own and beside him as well. So even though he worried about the team, he appreciated the honor and responsibility to lead them.

"Let's begin with prayer." Tears threatened to slip down Anthony's face, but he swallowed and began to pray with his whole heart.

No one knew what would come next and what battles lay ahead, personal or worldly.

All Anthony knew for certain was there would be more battles—some of the fiercest they would ever know.

# CHAPTER 36

All the Warriors in the team sat around the table, except Michael and Josh who were in different prisons.

The team knew very little about Josh, except that he had been moved to Slattersville. And Michael was still at the prison in Clanston.

"Okay, team." Anthony glanced at the group and gestured to the water and glasses placed around the table. "Deborah has furnished us with liquid to cool our parched throats. Feel free to help yourselves."

As the others passed the pitcher around he continued. "First we need to welcome our visitors, Chris and Tadd, to our meeting. As most of you know, these men haven't committed to anything. We don't even know if they are called. But they have both asked to be a part of this meeting just to listen to who we are and learn about the things that have occurred during our quest."

Murmurs of greeting came from the team members.

Then Anthony nodded to the newcomers. "If—at any time during the meeting—you don't feel this team and its pursuits are what God has in His plan for you, I encourage you to simply get up and leave."

He paused and looked at each of them, visitors and team alike. "This work is a special mission and is not for everyone. We all need to take it very seriously."

One by one, as his eyes focused on each person, they nodded that they understood.

"I feel God is preparing this group for times of spiritual warfare, possibly on a scale we have not yet encountered."

The visitors looked back at Anthony with widened eyes.

He felt the weight of the responsibility God had placed on him and wanted to convey it to the team. "I know others fight alongside us because I have seen the spiritual army encamped about us during several of these battles. Do you have any questions?"

"Who is this unseen army?"

"That is a good question, Chris. I believe it to be an army of angels God has commissioned to accompany us." Again Anthony glanced at each one. "The heavenly army are clothed with armor, and I've seen them kneeling at the Lord's presence and at His commands. You have to understand, this is the Lord's fight. We absolutely do not go into battle alone."

"Are you given armor as well?" Tadd asked.

Abby placed her hand over Tadd's. "I had armor the day I fought for you. But as far as I can tell, those who are not a part of the team are not able to see it."

"That's correct." Anthony leaned forward. "Only those who have been saved by the Lord and then called into service for Him can see what protects us."

"Okay." Tadd nodded. "That makes sense. So how do you receive the armor?"

"Good question." Abby settled back into her chair. "For me, I just stand in faith. Sometimes God tells me a battle is about to take place and not to fear because the battle is His. Then the armor just appears—usually the body armor suddenly surrounds me, the sword in one hand, the shield in the other, and then the helmet settles on my head."

"Yeah." Tadd's voice was filled with awe. "I couldn't see the battle but I heard God tell Abby that the battle was His. God must have seen something special in each of you."

Anthony shrugged. "I don't know about that. We are just common people."

"All of us started out as unsaved souls," Janet agreed. "We came to realize we were lost when the Holy Spirit convicted us of sin."

"Exactly. Some, like my sister Janet, were Christians long before the team began."

Janet continued the narrative. "He seems to send us to others in their trouble to help them. But only after each of us came to accept the Lord, did He call us and allow us to go into battle for each other."

"But at least you knew God had your back," said Chris.

"Yes, but during some of the battles several of us were wounded, and during others, we didn't have a scratch on us at the finish."

"So, it is still a leap of faith?" Tadd asked.

Anthony nodded. "Very much so. The only way to defeat our enemies—the demons that plague us—is to have faith, stand strong and call on the name of Jesus."

"This is so amazing," Chris said.

"All of the battles were actually His. I battled for Michael. Then three warriors, Abby, Michael and Janet battled for Josh. And later Josh battled for Abby."

"And yesterday I battled for you." Abby reached over and squeezed Tadd's forearm. "The team looks out for each other."

Anthony raised his eyebrows at Abby. "You haven't told us the details about that one yet."

"That's when I heard God talking to her." Tadd glanced at Abby. "From what I could hear she fought a nasty enemy."

"They are all nasty," Anthony agreed. "Okay, now, let's talk about where we are as far as battle plans. We have Josh in prison in Slattersville."

Tadd leaned forward. "Excuse me, but did you say Slattersville?"

"Yep. I think that's where we are all going to be eventually. Did I hear Abby say something about you going there to work, Tadd?"

"Yes." Tadd nodded. "That's why I asked. "Wow. Do you think it's a move of God?"

"Everything is a move of God," Chris spoke up. "Everything I have ever done in my ministry with children was done from God's point of view."

The team murmured amen and nodded.

"Chris, sounds like you might be interested in spiritual warfare." Anthony searched the other man's face.

"If God calls, I'm available." Chris's words rang with conviction. "I am truly inspired by your stories and want to be part of everything that God is doing here."

"Great. Make as much time as possible in prayer, to stay in God's Word, and to listen for the voice of the Holy Spirit. That's the way you are called, if God desires it."

Chris nodded.

"That goes for you too, Tadd. And for the rest of us as well," Anthony said. "As most of you know, I have been planning on moving here permanently. Only I don't know if Becky will want to do that, and I really need my family close. Ben needs me, too. I will talk with her about all this in the morning." Pray God she would, but who knew? Only God. And only God could plant that desire within his wife.

"Chris, Tadd, we'll all be praying for you and what God desires," Anthony assured the two men.

They glanced at each other and then back at Anthony and nodded in agreement.

"Let's also spend time in fervent prayer for all of our families and how they will deal with these changes. Then we will meet here again, tomorrow evening.

~*~

Upon returning to the cell, Viper climbed back in his bunk and curled up as before.

Josh eyed his cellmate and wondered if he could persuade him to talk. "Uh, Viper, how did you get that name?"

There was no immediate answer. In fact two or three minutes of silence passed.

"I coiled my way upward in this town."

"I see."

Viper glared at him. "No you don't see. Some knows all that goes on in this hellhole of a town, and I am one of them. Just because I'm in here don't even matter. I am still the King Snake, and you could be a rat. You know what snakes do to rats, don't you?"

Josh backed away. He did not say another word to Viper that night, but he sure talked a lot to God.

## CHAPTER 37

The two women enjoyed iced tea on the patio where they sat in folding chairs overlooking the garden.

Becky appreciated the special touch Deborah had with flowers and vegetables. She'd never tried to do much in the yard at their place in New York. Of course, if Anthony stayed away she might have to.

Ben pranced around the yard, munching on a ripe tomato as Anthony appeared from the other side of the house. Ben ran toward his dad with juice dripping down his chin. He held out the red vegetable.

"Dad, look what Mrs. Deborah gave to me."

Anthony nodded at Ben, tousled his hair, and glanced toward Becky. "Can we talk, honey?"

Rising from her chair, Deborah held her hand toward Ben. "Let's carry the rest of the vegetables we picked this morning into the house. We can show them to your Aunt Janet. I bet she would like one of these tomatoes as well."

"Okay." Ben scampered ahead of Deborah toward the house.

"Thanks, Deborah," Anthony called to her retreating back.

Her husband was still just as handsome as ever.

Becky was glad they'd come. But the looming conversation worried her somewhat.

Anthony went to the chair Deborah had vacated and sat. "Honey, I wondered if you'd given any more thought about leaving New York and moving here to be with me."

Becky hesitated, looked out over the garden and then back at him. "Anthony, being a new Christian is overwhelming to me. It's a whole new experience, and I'm trying to decide what God wants me to do."

"Do you really think He doesn't want our family to be together? It's not like I expect us to live in this little guest cottage permanently. We'll have our own home, I promise."

"To tell you the truth, I am a little afraid, and I feel like I need to take it slow."

"I can appreciate that. But—"

"Your life consists of demons and battles. Mine is just reading my Bible and learning to pray."

"I understand. And—"

"No, Anthony, I don't think you do understand. I want to be around the Christian friends who I know, and who I can trust to help me."

"Becky, I know you will love the church Janet and I have found here. Abby's church. It's much like the one we left in New York."

"You aren't listening. I want to be able to attend church in the community with which I am already familiar. I want to stay at my job for now and let

Ben attend the small school he is used to, at least, until I know whether God wants me to move."

Anthony's smile faded. "Oh, Becky, I wanted you and Ben with me. I miss you both so much. You don't seem to understand how I long for the two of you."

"This is not really about what I want or what you want. It's about what God wants from both of us." *Couldn't he see she was hurting too?*

"I'm sure they need Estheticians in Ohio. Your special talent with skin care will find a place here."

*Oh how the man knew how to push her buttons.* "I can't move until I know it's truly His will."

Anthony stood and turned from her.

"I know it's not what you wanted to hear, and I'm sorry."

"Forget it," her husband said abruptly. He stalked toward the house.

Becky frowned and got up as well. "Guess it's time to go." A tear slipped down her cheek as she headed toward the house to collect Ben, say goodbye and thank Deborah for her hospitality.

*Why would her husband never truly listen to her? To get to the heart of her needs?*

When she entered the house Janet was playing a game with Ben and obviously letting him win.

"Where's Deborah?" Becky asked.

"She had an appointment, so I got to spend time with my favorite nephew."

"Aunt Janet, I'm your only nephew," Ben rebuked her with a grin.

"You'd still be my favorite if I had a dozen." Janet told him, giving him a pat on the hand.

Becky glanced at Anthony who leaned against the counter, pretending to watch the game. She could tell by the glazed look in his eyes, he was preoccupied with all that they had said to each other.

Chris watched their game too, but had looked at Becky when she came in.

"So, Chris. Are you ready to head on back?"

"Well, Mrs. Becky, thank you so much for bringing me here, but I have decided to stay for a few days."

"You're welcome for the ride, of course," Becky said. "But are you really staying in Ohio?"

"Yes, Mrs. Deborah mentioned that I was welcome to continue using her extra bedroom until I decided what I wanted to do. At this point, I am leaning toward staying for a while. I can get by with the few clothes I brought with me. And, of course, I can get more at one of the local stores if I need to."

"Okay." Becky sighed. "Hey, Ben, we need to get rolling so we can get home before midnight."

"Aw, Mom," he whined. "I don't want to leave Dad."

"Ben, listen to your Mom," Anthony said. "Get busy and help Aunt Janet put the game away."

# Awareness

With a frown on his face, Ben started gathering up the game parts.

Becky caught Anthony's eye, and he managed a smile.

Encouraged, she smiled back. "Walk me to the apartment to get my luggage?"

"Sure." He moved to the door and opened it for her.

They moved together across the front porch and down the steps toward the guest cottage.

"I'm sorry I spoke to you so abruptly in my disappointment. I love you, and hope to someday have you and Ben close."

"I know. I love you too, and we will pray about it some more."

Anthony grabbed her bags, and she took Ben's lighter ones. They companionably headed out to the car, and even her husband's mood seemed to lighten.

When they reached the car, Becky stood on her toes and kissed him.

"Be safe," he whispered.

"We will. God will take care of us."

Anthony kissed her again and helped her get into the car.

Ben came running out of the house and grabbed his dad's arms. "Bye, Dad. See you later alligator."

"After a while, crocodile." Anthony teased back, as he helped Ben open his car door and fasten his seatbelt.

With a wave to her husband Becky put the car in reverse, backed down the drive, and pulled the car onto the street, knowing she was doing the right thing.

She'd no more gotten used to the idea of what was happening in Clanston, and then Deborah mentioned her husband's cellmate, another member of the team, had been moved to a prison in Slattersville.

Last night, while waiting for Anthony to return to the guest cottage, Becky had used Janet's laptop in the team's office to find out more about Slattersville. What she learned worried her.

The town was full of mystery. Would Anthony want to move there next?

~*~

Anthony walked toward the house, devastated.

Janet met him on the porch and he expected her to give him some sympathy and try to cheer him up.

"I wanted to tell you, I feel God calling me to help Pastor Joe. I sense he's depressed about his illness and having to give up the leadership of his church. I think the poor man needs some rescuing."

This was not what he'd expected to come out of his sister's mouth. "You hardly know the man, and he has a son who is running things now. Are you sure you heard that call from God, or is this a good way to get closer to the son?"

# Awareness

Janet frowned and glanced sideways at Anthony. "All the battles don't have to be fought with you at the center, brother dear."

*Ouch.* Anthony opened his mouth to spout a sarcastic comment back to his sister. *What in the world is wrong with you?* He wanted to say. Oh how he wanted to spit the words out. But something held him back.

"Look, Anthony," Janet continued, "I have a personal life too. You have Becky and Ben, but I am alone. And for your information, I don't like it."

Shame hit him right where it hurt. How could he? Anthony put his arm around her shoulders. "Ah, sis. You're not alone, we're here for you. We're all your family."

"You're talking about the team. Well, sometimes having brothers and sisters is not enough."

"Guess what, sis? When you put it that way, I have a wife and a son. But as you can see, I'm still alone."

Janet abruptly turned and walked back into the house, leaving Anthony standing there shaking his head.

# CHAPTER 38

**D**r. Sandra Beazel stood at one end of the waiting area and beckoned her patient. "You can come on back, Mrs. Reeves."

Deborah timidly stood. She made her way past the fashion magazines and overstuffed chairs in the waiting area and joined the psychologist in a hall which looked like it could go on for miles.

She followed the doctor into a plush office and sat down on a couch that was both colorful and comfortable.

"You have a lovely office," Deborah said with a shaky smile.

"Yes, it is. It was decorated by some fashionable PHD who had it before me." Dr. Beazel's laugh was pleasant and gave Deborah a comfortable sensation. "And please call me, Sandra."

"All right, and my name is Deborah." Her eyes swept around the room and back to Sandra's face. "I feel a little awkward coming here. I've never been to a psychologist before."

"Don't think of me by my title. Let's just be two friends as you share a little about yourself and your situation."

"That sounds good. Let's see. I've been working at

the same place for about ten years. I'm married, no children. My husband, Michael, was arrested and put in jail several months ago for DUI."

Sandra held Debora's eye and nodded. "I can see how that would be stressful."

"Yes. It was his third offense, so he's serving a six months term."

"And you miss him."

"Well, before that he was very abusive to me and had anger issues. But since becoming a Christian, he put that behind him and has really been kind and gentle toward me, so, yes, I miss him."

"I sense there is more though?"

"Yes. You see, he's been more agitated and frustrated since he's been incarcerated." Deborah stopped talking and put her trembling hands up to her face. "Now I'm afraid. I cannot go back to the abuse. I just can't."

Sandra put her hand on Deborah's arm, "I understand. It's a hard thing to be separated from someone you care about and also feel the brunt of all that anger."

Deborah looked into Sandra's soft, caring eyes. "Thank you. "I needed to hear that someone understands."

"Let me ask you a little more about your husband."

"All right."

"Does he have any special interests? Can you tell

me what he was passionate about before he was sent to prison?"

Deborah looked away a moment and then back at the doctor. "He was passionate about the team."

"The team?" the doctor questioned. "What sort of team are you talking about?"

"You might—uh, I started to say you might think I'm crazy."

Both of them laughed at that.

Then Deborah explained about Anthony coming to the hospital and fighting the demons that had troubled both her and Michael. How it led to Michael's conversion and his becoming part of God's team of warriors.

"I don't know everything that happened after that, but I do know the team is at the center of Michael's existence."

"It sounds exciting. But I'm wondering where you fit into all of this. Are you not somewhere in the center of his existence?"

Deborah looked down at her hands and twisted her wedding band around her finger. "Well, I guess the jail sentence has taken care of that aspect of our relationship. Of course, I don't think the team has caused the separation. And really, I have enjoyed having them with me during this time. The team has been a comfort to me as well as Michael."

"Deborah, do you love Michael?" the doctor inquired.

## Awareness

"Yes. Yes I do. I just want things to be back the way they were after he accepted Jesus. But I don't know how to get there from here." She looked back up at the doctor.

"Don't worry, I will help you find your way back. But, I want to meet this team you told me about. That might help me understand a bit better where you are at the moment."

"There is a meeting tomorrow evening if you'd like to come. I'll jot down the address."

"Sounds good," the doctor replied with a smile.

~*~

That evening Anthony lay in his bed, looking up at the ceiling. Becky was so determined to stay in New York. She had not really given him a chance to explain anything else.

How he had wanted to share with her about his dreams of a law firm of his own. He wanted her to be excited for him, to dream with him, but she definitely had not been in the mood to hear about it this morning.

He mentally kicked himself because he hadn't yet looked into openings for Dermatologists needing Becky's specialty.

How could he survive without his wife and son here beside him?

*I wonder where I could go this time of night to get a drink.*

Old habits and hang-ups nagged at his mind and

body.

*If only I could just have one drink, I probably could relax and get some sleep.*

The phone rang. It was Janet.

"Anthony, I'll be home late," she said without offering a reason.

"Okay. Is everything alright?"

"Sure. I'm a big girl, you know."

"I know, Janet, I'm just concerned. We need to talk."

"Later. Tomorrow maybe. Don't wait up for me. Goodnight."

Anthony looked at the silent phone and slapped his hand against his forehead. *What is going on with her? Boy, do I need that drink.*

But instead of getting up and hunting for a bar he pounded his pillow.

It was time to check out Slattersville, not only for himself, but, as a good leader, Anthony knew he owed it to the whole team.

~*~

"Pastor Joe, can you tell me why you feel so down?" Janet put her hand on his old and withered one.

The elderly gentleman seemed unable to speak for a moment.

She waited.

"I don't know. I wish I did. I've been the pastor at this church for thirty years, and I just feel so unhappy. I'm dissatisfied and disappointed with myself."

"Have you talked to God about it?"

Her heart hurt at the pained expression which crossed the elderly pastor's face.

"I haven't been able to talk to God much lately. And I'm ashamed about that," he whispered.

"You don't need to be ashamed. God understands."

"Does He? I rather think He might condemn me."

"Let me pray for you." Janet took his hand in hers. "God, how thankful I am to have recently become acquainted with Pastor Joe. We're both thankful that we know you love and forgive each and every one of us. Please comfort this man of God tonight and ease his doubts."

He latched onto her hand, when she'd finished praying. "Will you come back and talk to me again? Pray with me like this?"

"Sure, I will." Again she prepared to leave. "I'll come back tomorrow. Now think about talking to God yourself. He's always near to us, you know, and ready to listen."

He smiled and nodded.

"You rest now."

She let herself out of his little apartment, and as Janet walked away, she heard someone following her. She stopped and tilted her head to hear better. Sure enough, the footsteps kept coming.

Janet whirled, putting her hand over her heart. "Robert, you scared me to death," she exclaimed as she recognized him.

"I'm sorry, Janet. I heard someone walking near dad's apartment, and I decided to see who was visiting. Forgive me for startling you." Then he grinned "When I came out here I didn't know I would run into such a pretty lady."

"Compliments will get you nowhere." Janet cringed. *I can't believe I just said that to a pastor.*

Her cheeks burned, and she knew she was blushing. She hoped Robert couldn't see well by the subdued light in the parking area.

"Here let me walk you to your car."

It felt good to be walking next to a man. To feel his strength. It had been a long time since she'd been escorted anywhere.

When she reached for the door handle of her car, Reverend Robert caught her hand and squeezed it. "I hope you'll come back to visit dad again soon. Let me know when you're coming, and I'll cook something for us."

She slipped into the car and started it. As she pulled out of the parking area, she glanced in the rear-view mirror. He was still standing there watching her drive away.

Her heart sang all the way home.

~*~

Josh heard the sound of shoe clad feet running

down a paved street.

In an old warehouse in Slattersville, a pane of glass shattered.

A man stood in the midst of a group of rag-tag youth and spoke in a raspy voice, "Anthony, you will be broken like that glass—into a thousand pieces, and no one will know your name except for me."

An evil noise emanated from the demon— Apollyon—somewhere between laughter and a scream.

Josh stood frozen in place as a knife glimmered in the hand of someone clothed completely in black.

The knife holder circled around Josh and came behind him in an instant. He felt the tip of the knife blade touching his back.

Suddenly a bright light burst into the surrounding area. A thundering voice spoke out of the night. "Do not fear. Tell him what you know, Warrior."

Tell what to whom? Josh woke drenched in sweat, and his heart raced.

Minutes later, breathing restored to normal by the steady snoring of his cellmate, Josh pondered what the dream could mean.

He needed to know the answer soon. He had to talk to Anthony, and he had to press Viper for information—at least one more time.

## CHAPTER 39

The next morning Anthony clocked his travel time at forty-five minutes when he passed the Slattersville city limit sign.

With the main road so desolate, he wasn't surprised most of the businesses appeared to be closed. Boards covered the windows, and he saw no people anywhere.

He circled the block at the end of the street and encountered homes that also looked long deserted. Many windows were broken, and the grass was knee-high in most of the yards.

Old cars, some with flat tires, were parked here and there, the tires surrounded by tall grass and weeds.

It was hard to imagine anyone had ever lived in this ghost-town.

However, one gas station seemed to be open at the center of it all, and one dingy little hole-in-the-wall had a sign which simply said EAT hanging on the outside wall, while another sign below it boasted OPEN 24 HOURS.

If worse came to worse Anthony could stop there for information.

After driving a couple more blocks, he saw a

medical building of some kind on the next corner. A few cars parked nearby even looked drivable.

Perhaps the town wasn't totally abandoned after all.

What looked like a lawyer's shingle which had been hanging on the front of another building, had fallen down and was now resting at an angle on the concrete of the front entrance.

The empty office looked about the right size for the team headquarters. And really, they needed to quit taking advantage of Deborah's hospitality.

Making a decision to check it out, Anthony parked in front of the abandoned lawyer's office, got out, walked carefully through the tall grass, and up the steps.

The boards gave a little at his firm footsteps, and he stepped the rest of the way more gingerly, stopping abruptly when he noticed the door had a padlock on it.

Anthony tried peeping through the grimy glass at the window, but could see nothing.

Disappointed, he returned to his car wondering where to find more information about the empty office, but as he reached for the door handle, the old medical building caught his attention. *Why not?* He headed toward it.

As he reached the door to the front of the old building, he heard a scraping noise. Someone pulled on the door from the other side, and when it opened, a sober faced girl stood there. She looked to be ten-years-old, and about as gloomy as her surroundings.

"Hi," Anthony said with what he hoped was a reassuring smile.

She silently turned toward someone beyond his line of vision.

He heard a sound like the cocking of a gun and ducked against the outside wall.

"Who's there?" a female voice yelled.

"I'm Anthony Markson. Inquiring about the building next door."

"Don't know nothin' about it," the voice filtered through a crack in the door. "You better not be poking around here this time of day. You get your head blowed off."

"Sorry." Anthony back-stepped and fast-walked down the steps toward his car.

Maybe Becky had been right. This was a dangerous place, and it was still daylight.

Originally he'd wanted to look for the prison while he was here, but now he just wanted to get back to Clanston. At least he wouldn't risk staring down the barrel of a rifle. Anthony jumped into his car and drove away.

~*~

Across the road from the deserted office, someone had watched all the events that occurred, observed the black and grey smoke surrounding the buildings, and smelled the stench in the air.

# Awareness

The watcher shook his head and wondered where he fit—if he fit at all—into this mounting whirlwind of a nightmare.

He had long since put away his sword, and there seemed to be no one strong enough to do battle now.

With a sigh of despair, he headed on down the street, turned at the corner and disappeared.

~*~

That evening when Josh returned from supper, he found Viper already in the cell, lying in his normal fetal position on his bunk.

"Uh, Viper. I'd like to ask you a few questions."

He didn't get an answer, but Viper's head moved.

"Where do you come from?"

Viper dove off the lower bunk and grabbed Josh by the throat, "How many times do I have to tell you to shut your trap?"

Just at that moment a guard came down the hall with another prisoner at his side. "Stay here. Don't move."

Then he clomped to the cell. "Viper. Put him down, now."

Viper gave the guard a cold stare, but he released Josh.

Josh landed on his back on the cold hard concrete. His throat burned as with fire, and he struggled to breathe. Weaker than a newborn baby, he had no strength to move from the floor where he had fallen.

The other prisoner, standing outside the cell smirked. "Don't worry, Viper. When they move you to your next cell, maybe Mr. Stupid will like his new cellmate better."

Josh was weak, but not so weak that he didn't wonder about the words the other prisoner had thrown at them. *What did he mean? Why did they move Viper so often?*

"Yeah," Viper retorted to the other prisoner, "You're right, Sammie, let's see if he asks Big Jax all these stupid questions."

At the sound of Big Jax's name the trembling began. Josh glanced at the guard, terror raging through his body, but he was unable to speak a word.

The guard glanced at him, then shrugged and walked on down the hall with the other prisoner.

Cold sweat popped out on Josh's forehead. *Oh God, how could you let them move my enemy here?*

Wasn't this why they'd moved him from the Clanston Prison?

Josh turned his head and looked right into the evil grinning face of Viper. For the first time Josh noticed the snake's incisor teeth resembled fangs.

Viper threw back his head and hissed a raspy, mocking laugh as he lay back onto his bunk.

.

# CHAPTER 40

Doctor Beazel had been a psychologist for ten years now and a Christian for nearly twenty. She had many patients who suffered in their minds and bodies, but they'd taught her a lot.

In her studies, demons had seemed a result of a psychological imbalance. However Sandra's practice had eventually proved her wrong. She'd concluded most people who appeared to be afflicted, suffered from a life lived without God's direction.

And now she'd discovered a group of people who seemed to be addressing demons head-on. Curiosity and excitement built as the time drew nearer for the meeting.

Sandra had carefully followed the directions to Deborah's home in Clanston. As she pulled into the driveway, her hostess waved from the window and came running out to greet her.

Once inside, Deborah introduced the doctor to the team members who had assembled.

"Hey, everyone, this is Dr. Beazel." Deborah raised her voice to gain their attention, and then she called out each name around the table for Sandra's benefit.

"It's so nice to meet all of you. Like I told Deborah yesterday, please, call me Sandra. I am glad you allowed me to meet with you today."

"Welcome, Sandra. Glad to have you with us." Anthony held out his hand. "Please have a seat."

He pulled up two chairs. "And Deborah, join us also, if you will."

Deborah nodded and slipped into the chair beside Sandra. "Thank you."

"Okay, guys, let's begin." Anthony rubbed his hand across his forehead. "I need to tell you about my experience today at Slattersville."

"You went without us?" Abby stuck out her lower lip, pretending to pout. Then she grinned. "Well, let's hear all about it."

He made a silly face back at her. "If only you'd been there, maybe you could have faced what I did. Then I could have stayed in the car." His expression turned serious. "It wasn't at all what I expected. In fact, it was quite dangerous."

"We've seen dangerous." Abby threw her head and her pony tail swung back and forth. "How was this different?"

"For one thing, I had a gun cocked and pointed at me."

"Not again, Anthony." Janet's voice wavered with fear. "What about your armor. Didn't the Lord fight for you?"

"It's okay, I'm fine." He reached over and patted Janet's shoulder. "But this is not going to be an easy task. I didn't see much in the way of people there, and many homes and businesses are in shambles."

"How disappointing."

He nodded. "I did find a building that appeared to have been a medical center at one time, but when I approached, the person inside was not about to give me information." Anthony let his gaze light on each one around the table.

"I only wanted to inquire about the building next door to it. It looked to have been a lawyer's office— or at least, I saw a lawyer's shingle there. Anyway when I went to the door of the old clinic and knocked, a little girl opened it."

"Was she in danger? Do you think you were sent to help her?"

"I can't answer that. But somewhere in the darkness inside, someone with a gun didn't give me too kind of a welcome."

"You shouldn't have gone alone, Anthony." Janet spoke sharper than usual.

"You're probably right. At any rate I really don't know much more than I did before I went. I didn't know who to contact about the unoccupied lawyer's building, so I left."

"Maybe I can help with that, if I may," Sandra spoke up then.

As one the puzzled group turned their eyes and their attention to her.

"Please do. We need all the help we can get," Anthony encouraged her to continue.

"When you said the name of Slattersville, I immediately knew why God brought me here today. You see, I used to have a practice in that same medical building."

"Wow. Talk about coincidences."

"You're right. There was a lawyer's practice beside the medical center. In fact I know the man who owns the building, and I can probably get you a key if you want."

Anthony looked at her in amazement. "God is really working in our behalf this evening. Thanks, Sandra."

"Anthony, what are you thinking about doing with the building?" Chris asked.

"Well, that's one of the things I wanted to speak with all of you about tonight." Anthony again glanced at each one. "I thought the building might make a great meeting place one day."

The rest of the team looked at him in amazement, questions and excitement shining from their eyes.

"We need to quit taking advantage of Deborah's hospitality," he continued.

"But I like having you here," Deborah protested. "It helps me not to be alone while Michael is not here."

"This is not a done deal, of course. It's only a dream. Just like my other dream."

"Tell us about your other dream, Anthony."

# Awareness

"I think you all know I was a senior partner with Dickerson, Markson, and Clark Law Offices in New York."

The others nodded.

"When God sent me to Ohio, I resigned and have some money coming to me. I would really like to open my own law practice here in Clanston."

"Now that is good news, my friend." Abby's grin was infectious.

Chris got up and shook his hand, and Tadd followed.

"Thanks all of you, but I want to make sure you know Slattersville is a dangerous place. We all need to think about this and pray, because I want each one of you to realize what you will be getting into just by going there."

"This is heavy stuff," Tadd said.

"That's a word Michael used." Anthony chuckled at the memory. "I know God has a plan for Slattersville, because Josh is already there. Tadd, you will be working there soon, and now Sandra has come to give us the information we need to get started."

"Has God spoken directly to you about this, Anthony?" Janet asked in an unusually quiet voice.

Anthony glanced over at her, "Well, no, not directly, but look at all the circumstances. Surely this vision is from Him. In God, there are no coincidences, but *God-incidences*." He turned to get assurance from the others.

Everyone nodded except Janet, who remained quiet and pensive.

"Anyway, please all of you pray about this. I really want us to go there as soon as possible, and we need to visit Josh while we are there."

After more discussion, the team decided to go to Slattersville together for the specific purpose of exploring the now abandoned office building Anthony hoped one day would be their headquarters and to find the prison where Josh was now located.

Sandra agreed to contact the owner and get a key. Then she promised to call and they would all meet at Deborah's and ride to Slattersville together.

With God's blessing, this would all happen within the next few days.

# CHAPTER 41

Word on the prison grapevine said the doctors expected Big Jax to die at any moment. One week passed, then two, and still Big Jax remained unconscious.

Meanwhile Michael kept praying and reading his Bible.

"I have chosen Big Jax," the Lord said.

Those words made Michael straighten his back. "Really? The monster? You have chosen him?"

"My ways are not your ways."

"They sure aren't."

"I am preparing him even in his unconscious state."

"Okay. Okay. That's cool."

"It won't be long until he returns to this cell," the Spirit said. "And you have much to teach him."

"Yes, Lord," Michael said. Trepidation, faith, and courage mingled together inside of him.

~*~

When Big Jax finally woke up, the memory returned of being stabbed in his old cell block. Because of the uprising against him, he'd been transferred to a new cell but the face of his new mate eluded him.

The memory of a strange dream hovered also within him. Armor-clad, sword swinging warriors made war against a huge fire breathing dragon, and were victors in the battle.

And for some strange reason Big Jax could feel the taste of metal in his mouth.

~*~

Two days later when Michael returned from the evening meal, Big Jax was in the cell, lying on his bunk.

With pounding heart, Michael hesitated just inside the cell. A voice behind him spoke, and he turned.

"Hi Michael, is everything alright?" Janet stood there. To be sure, she was a welcome sight.

"The Spirit told us to come," Abby added just the right words to sooth his spirit.

"Sure. Big Jax just got back, and he seems pretty weak yet."

Michael turned to his cellmate. "We were worried about you. Are you feeling okay now?"

Big Jax looked at Janet and Abby then back at Michael. "I can't remember much. Do I know you?"

"I've taken care of you in the infirmary," Abby said. "I'm Abby by the way and the other lady is Janet."

"You had the doctors chattering," Janet said. "But you must be feeling better if they let you come back to the cell."

# Awareness

"Why don't we pray before you leave?" Michael suggested.

Big Jax mumbled and rolled over, effectively putting his back side towards them.

"Thank you, Lord, for your servant Michael, and for his cellmate. Be with Big Jax just now and heal the wounds of his body and mind. Reconcile him back to you, Lord. In Jesus' name. Amen."

After Abby and Janet left, Big Jax rolled over and faced Michael. "One of those women prayed for me?"

"That's right."

"That was a first." Big Jax squinted his eyes, evidently puzzled. "Why would you do that? You Christian?"

"Yes, we are," Michael said.

~*~

A huge foot stomped on Big Jax's neck, squeezing the breath from his body.

Sticky blood surrounded him. He screamed for help, but he was alone. Nobody would hear, let alone rescue him.

"Be with Big Jax just now and heal the wounds of his body and mind. Reconcile him back to you, Lord. In Jesus' name. Amen."

The prayer of reconciliation from the two young women stirred his soul.

"Do you want to live or die?" another voice asked.

"I want to live," Big Jax said. "Of course, I want to

live."

A dark force tugged on his legs and pulled him further into the darkness. "No. You are mine. I already own your soul."

With pounding heart, Big Jax jerked awake and sat up in his cot glad to be out of the dream and alive. He cracked his head on the upper bunk.

Rubbing his head, he punched the board supporting the top bunk with his fist. "Hey man! You awake?"

"I am now," Michael said. "What did you want to talk about at 3:00 o'clock in the morning?"

"Is it that early?"

"Are you all right Big Jax?"

"I don't know man, I just had a nightmare, and I cannot understand anything of this. I am worried. I have never given a thought about my life, but I don't wanna die."

"The Lord revealed your dream to me," Michael assured him. "He gave me words to tell you. That is, if you want to hear them."

"The what? What Lord are you talking about? A Drug Lord? You a dealer or something?"

"You know better than that," Michael said. "But I do know all about your dream."

"Nah, don't kid man. That kind of stuff makes me mad. I haven't even told you about my dream yet."

"Well, let's see. You were choked by a monster foot, lying in a bed of your own blood"

"Y—yeah," Big Jax said.

"And the Lord offered you life."

"That was the Lord?"

"Yes, Jesus Christ wants to give you life."

"But, what about Botis?"

"The old dragon doesn't want to let you go, does he?"

"So, now what, Michael? Ain't that your name?"

"The Lord Jesus Christ, who died on the cross for you, is calling you out from the darkness to the light. And as I told you, and as you remember in your dreams, the darkness, Botis, is fighting over your soul. In fact, don't you remember how you got all these injuries and how you almost got killed?"

"Maybe. Kind of. So, you're sayin' I just need to accept your God?"

"Well, yes and no. I mean, yes, you just need to accept Him with all your heart. But no. He is not only my God, He is also yours, and He, my friend, is calling you.

"Big Jax," said the Elite Commander in an audible voice. "I am the Lord, God almighty. I have come to save you, and bring you from darkness to light. The question is do you want to have eternal life?"

"Yes, Lord," Big Jax said.

He turned to Michael. "I want to be saved. What do I have to do, Michael?"

"Just repeat after me: God, I know I have sinned against You and deserve punishment."

"Oh God forgive me," Big Jax prayed. "I have sinned against You, and I deserve to die."

"But Jesus Christ took the punishment I deserve." Michael continued to lead Big Jax in prayer. "So that through faith in Him I could be forgiven. I place my trust in You for salvation. Thank You for Your wonderful grace and forgiveness, the gift of eternal life. Amen."

Big Jax repeated the prayer, ending with, "Lord, please forgive me."

"My son," the Spirit answered. "You will no longer be called the dragon. I have given you a new name, and you will now be called The Decipher."

A new brother by his side, Michael spent the next hours discussing the Bible and everything he knew about Christ.

The rest of that night there was a party with much rejoicing in heaven for this new soul for the kingdom.

And in the cell there was peace and a restful sleep until the call for breakfast.

## CHAPTER 42

The time had come for Janet to make good on her promise to visit Pastor Joe again. And, of course, Robert's invitation to dinner the next time she visited his father wasn't a detriment.

She hadn't called Robert the past few times she had visited, but for some reason, this time, she could smell delicious aromas of supper cooking.

Before she could change her mind, Janet dialed the reverend's number.

"Hello?" a female voice answered the phone. *Perhaps one of the church ladies helping out?*

"Can I speak to Robert, please?"

"He's in the shower at the moment. Can I take a message?" the woman asked.

A creepy feeling washed over Janet's shoulders. *What was a woman doing at his house while he showered?*

"Just tell him Janet called to say I'm coming to visit Pastor Joe."

"Oh, sure. I'll let him know."

"Thanks." Janet snapped off the phone a little harder than usual. Then she shrugged it off. Likely there was a good explanation.

Putting the woman out of her mind, Janet

grabbed her bag and keys and took off for Pastor Joe's place.

Halfway to the pastor's home, her cell rang. She looked at the caller ID then picked up, "Hello?"

"Hi, Janet. This is Robert. Did you call?"

*Was his voice trembling?*

"Yes, I wanted you to know I'm on my way to see your dad."

"Why sure. Come right on. He'll be thrilled."

"Okay. I'll see him in a few minutes, unless—do you know if he already has other plans?"

"Oh, no, it will be fine." Robert didn't mention his own plans for the evening, or who the lady on the other end of the phone had been.

Twenty minutes later Janet pulled into the parking area and reached for the door handle. But before she could open it, a black sedan driven by a dark haired young woman whizzed past Janet's car and out of the lot. When she saw the woman's angry face, she was glad the driver hadn't glanced her way.

Frozen in place, she didn't move until the other vehicle was completely out of sight, and then she climbed out of her car and walked briskly to Pastor Joe's apartment.

When he answered the door, Janet was astonished to see the elderly gentleman looked even older than he had the day before.

Beyond him a dark cloud twisted, whirled, and spun about the room. Broken glass littered the floor.

Someone had had a heyday throwing lamps, dishes, and who knows what else.

"Pastor Joe, are you alright?"

"Come in, dear." The elderly pastor whispered as though he could barely talk.

As she stepped inside, he staggered, gave her one terrified look, and crumpled to the floor.

"Pastor Joe," she screamed and dashed toward him.

The pastor had a pulse, and he was still breathing but irregularly.

She left him then and went to the door to look for Robert, thinking he might be on his way over. But the man was nowhere to be seen.

As she picked up her phone to call 9-1-1, it was snatched from her hand by a force so powerful she could feel the wind blow against her body.

In the darkness, a huge pair of eyes blinked at her. She could barely make out the long arms and the hand which gripped her cell before the phone flew against the wall and shattered into pieces.

"You have entered Legion's territory." The poltergeist in the center of the cloud screamed with laughter.

"Do not be afraid," God spoke to her aloud. "This battle will be fierce, but I will fight with you as will the others."

She heard the clanging of metal and saw the heavenly warriors standing on each side of her.

Once again she was fully armored, holding her sword.

Before she was totally prepared, the cloud and wind came toward her screaming, "I will rule. You will see that I am the mighty one here."

There was no time to call out to the Lord. Janet felt herself being pulled into a whirlwind, spinning around and around and then being dropped to the floor.

Darkness blinded her, and she was out.

~*~

When Janet woke, her vision was fuzzy as if someone had put salve in her eyes. She lay flat on her back.

Was she still at Pastor Joe's house? Was he okay? She attempted to push herself into a sitting position. Someone had put her into a bed.

She had dressed carefully in case Robert had shown up at his father's house. Had her tangle with the whirlwind ripped her new gown? She gingerly touched her dress and realized from the feel of the fabric, someone had undressed her. Her heart raced. *Who?*

"Robert? Pastor Joe?" Janet called, frightened now.

Footsteps padded into the room.

Did Pastor Joe have linoleum or tile in his bedrooms? Janet was sure the living room had been carpeted.

# Awareness

"Who's there?" Janet didn't remember when her voice had been so squeaky.

"My name is Erin Ludwig," the woman's pleasant voice replied.

*The angry brunette from the parking lot? Or the woman who'd answered Roberts's phone?*

"Where am I?"

"You are at Clanston Memorial Hospital. I am your nurse today."

"Oh, are you that friend of Abby Power?"

"Yes, do you know her?"

"I just started attending her church. In fact, I was visiting the elderly Pastor Joe when—" Janet stopped speaking and glanced at the nurse. "What time is it?"

"You missed breakfast. Are you hungry? I can get you something."

"What day is it?"

"It's Friday. You and Pastor Joe were brought into the emergency room last night."

"I can't see."

"Yes, the doctor said your eyes were wind-burnt. That sometimes goes along with the decompression event of being caught in a tornado."

"Tornado?"

"Yes, and it must have been a small and localized one, as we have no other patients brought in from the storm as yet. I'm sorry to tell you your clothing has seen better days. What do you remember?"

"Very little. I do know my cell was destroyed. Do I have a phone in the room? Do you have Abby's number? Could you call her for me?"

## CHAPTER 43

It was a Saturday morning in late August. Anthony was out on his run when Sandra called his cell.

"Good morning, Anthony. I know this is short notice but I finally managed to reach the owner of the office building in Slattersville you're interested in seeing."

"Great. What did he say? Will he let us see the place?"

"Good news. I have the key. So what do you say? Want to try to run over there today?"

"That's not a problem. When are you available?"

"I can get away a little later this morning. If you can contact the others who want to go, I could meet you at Deborah's house."

"I'll be there for sure, Anthony said. "As soon as I get back from my run, I will call all the others."

Anthony stopped at the house and checked Janet's room, disappointed the door was still shut.

*So she was sleeping in.* He hadn't heard her little Honda Civic arrive last night, but since she was staying in the house now and he had been so tired. He'd gone to sleep without waiting up.

He knocked on his sister's door and waited for her answer. He pounded for a second time.

Still no answer.

His shoulders slumped. She must have already left to do something else. *I wish I could have spoken to her last night and knew what her plans were for today.*

He didn't knock again but mentioned the excursion to Chris, along with the news that he couldn't find Janet.

"I expected to see her at breakfast, but haven't caught a glimpse of her this morning either," Chris said.

Anthony shrugged and proceeded to call the other team members. He became more revved up about the trip as he talked to each one. Everyone he called could make it work and agreed to meet at the house at ten.

After he rang off from the last call, Anthony went to the apartment to grab a shower and dress.

While he and Chris waited for the others, Anthony answered the many questions Chris still had. As the minutes ticked away, he became more and more excited about what the day would hold.

A little before ten all the others had arrived, and except for a question or two about where Janet was everyone assumed they could do no more to contact her than Anthony had.

A twinge of worry ate at him, but he shook it off. He'd done all he could. Once we get to Slattersville, he'd give her a call.

The group piled into Anthony's new minivan and

reached the city limits in exactly forty-five minutes.

Anthony parked across the street because he wanted to speak to the team before they walked over to the building. He gestured for the others to join him in a circle.

"Here's the plan. We will go directly to the front entrance, unlock it, and go inside. Please be careful and follow me closely. Do not wander off by yourself."

After getting a nod from each of them, he gave a thumbs-up. "Okay, let's go."

"Ye have not because ye ask not," God spoke very clearly to Anthony's heart.

God's messages had always spoken positively in the past. But this message seemed to hold a negative tone. Was God trying to tell him something?

With the team's excitement behind him, the heat of the moment overwhelmed him. Running across the road with the others following behind, Anthony headed toward the building.

Sandra handed the key to him when they reached the entrance.

As Anthony turned the key in the lock, he heard distant laughter. He shrugged off the feeling of unease. God had never let him down in the past. Why would this day be any different?

With a quick glance at his team, he was proud to be part of this group that had been called by God. When they finished here the town wouldn't know what had hit it.

Anthony placed the opened padlock into the loop, leaving the latch flipped open.

He handed Sandra the key, pushed open the door, and stepped over the threshold.

He stopped dead in his tracks. *How weird.* The windows had no curtains or blinds over them, and yet the room was very black.

"I can't see a thing," Chris remarked in his distinctive New York brogue.

Anthony knew the sun was shining outside. How strange that no light filtered into the darkened building. He reached for the light switch and flipped it with no change. *Duh.* Of course. The electricity was off.

The front door slammed shut. A click sounded throughout the room as if the padlock was latched.

Abby cried out.

Anthony tried to turn in her direction, but it did him no good. He could not see a thing.

"Duck," Tadd yelled. "Something's flying around in here. This room must be full of birds or maybe even bats."

"I hope it's not bats." The fear in Sandra's voice was real and by the sound of it, she stood nearby.

"Wait." Was that panic in her voice now? "I have a mini flashlight in my pocket." Sandra had no sooner turned it on then something slapped it out of her hand and it clattered on the floor.

Eyes. The tiny beam showed dozens of pairs of eyes blinking at them. Then, eerily, the light went out.

"I slipped," Sandra's scream rent the air. "I'm falling into a hole. Ouch, my ankle."

Anthony felt the air stir around him. Where was Sandra?

"Tadd?" Abby's voice was cautious.

Something crashed to the floor.

"Abby, are you okay?" Tadd questioned. "Where did you go?"

There was no answer.

Anthony stained to see through the darkness. "Abby, do you have your armor and sword?" he yelled.

"No," was her very weak reply.

"Abba Father, we need you," Anthony shouted.

Suddenly an audible flurry of wings surrounded Anthony. Amazingly, his sword appeared in his hand, and he swung his arm wildly. Another scream split the air. What on earth was happening?

If only he could get close to the wall. At least he could get his bearings, but there was nothing. Empty space as far as he could reach.

The demonic creatures began to screech, and the foul odor of decaying and rotting meat permeated the room.

Anthony stood erect, his head tilted, trying to catch the direction from where he heard the sound of dragging feet. The screams of the flying creatures got louder and louder until he wanted to cover his ears from the pain.

They'd failed. The realization struck him with a blow. They'd come on this mission unprepared to face the likes of Apollyon.

"Lord God, please help us. Don't forsake us," Anthony cried out, tears pouring from his eyes, the sadness in his heart almost more than he could bear.

He paused to gather strength. Were the screams diminishing? "God forgive us and save us. We can't do this without You. Lord, we need you."

A small ray of light appeared at the bottom of a slit under the door making the flashlight visible at his feet. Anthony picked it up and flicked the light around the floor, searching for Abby.

She lay in a pool of blood, her arm sliced open and claw marks on her face. Anthony stared at this precious team member. *Could it be vampire bats attacking them?*

Tadd, kneeling next to Abby, tried to stop the bleeding in her arm. "She's barely breathing. And my hands are shaking so badly, I can hardly apply pressure."

Feeling as helpless as he'd ever experienced, Anthony searched the room for the other members of the team.

Sandra began to pull herself out of the hole she'd fallen into.

## Awareness

Chris lay on his side, bruised and battered, but his chest moved with each breath. Thank God he was alive.

Anthony stood gazing at this room where something evil and horrific had taken place. His eyes ached from the strain of trying to see through the darkness. This battle had not gone well. Why had God let the evil prevail against them? For sure, the team needed to learn from this tragedy.

Sandra hobbled over to him. Her mouth opened as if she would say something reassuring. But no words came.

"Okay, team," Anthony said. "We really need to set some guidelines. Up to this point we have winged it somewhat because God initially spoke to us individually on so many things."

Again, the others nodded their understanding.

"It's time to go home and regroup. We need to repent before God and ask Him to show us where we have gone wrong and lead us back to His way."

Anthony walked to the door and turned the knob, but when the door refused to open, he remembered. The click. The possibility of being locked in this evil place.

"Please dear God, help us get out of here!"

~*~

And all this time, someone stood just beyond the parked cars and watched as the team shoved the door open and went inside.

He saw them standing, kneeling, crawling and saw two who were unable to move. He knew what they had been through and why. As he remembered his own past, it was hard to watch them butchered by the demon vampire bats.

Life had not been easy for Daniel Samuels. He had lived under devastating circumstances, had been desperate and made many mistakes. But now he could see the error of his ways, the damage he'd done, and the hurt he'd given.

His heart felt as if it would burst from his chest. His body trembled as something burned inside of him. Tears gushed down his rugged face.

Was this it? Was he dying? He'd felt this way many years ago. Before he had retired from God's plan. *He was too old,* he'd said in his heart. *This mission is for young men.*

Pride had driven him to this place, and Daniel looked up the sky

"Lord, I know there is no one like You. Forgive my foolishness for thinking I could retire from your army. Please embrace me once again."

"You are restored my son; your new mission begins now," God spoke with an audible voice as before.

Once again peace resided in Daniel's heart, and his mind became rational again. He was fully restored.

God told him his mission would involve this

team who seemed filled with such a great purpose. Helping them to not make these same disastrous choices was God's plan for him.

But could he say yes? He trembled at the implications.

Would they even listen if he did?

Had he?

What if he messed up again? But maybe they would be much wiser than he had been.

Was he the right one to do this?

Finally he gave up the struggle, he surrendered full and complete. Someone far greater than he would make that call.

If God wanted him, he would answer.

"Daniel, you have made the right decision, and I have changed your name. You will now be called *The Emissary*. I have given you the gift of prophecy, and you will deliver my message to the team. Your past experience will guide them in their quests." God's voice was strong, his omnipotence unquestioning.

"Time for battle," said the Elite Commander.

The Emissary once again had his sword and armor ready for battle, with his new name written on his right upper arm *The Emissary*.

The spiritual army became visible. "This is a very tough battle. Time is of the essence," The Commander Elite told the army. "You will intervene and fight alongside of *the Emissary* before it is too late. End this quickly."

*The Emissary* took long strides down the street toward God's enemy, Apollyon.

With one sweep, *the Emissary*—who had not taken a stand in a very long time—ended the Enemy's game. And for the first time the spiritual army stood and fought alongside him.

The team never knew what had happened, or how the door became unlocked, but *the Emissary* did, and now, someone needed to tell them.

Dear Reader,

I hope you enjoyed the first book in the series: *The Hero Within: Awareness.*

I have to tell you, I really love this hero story. Many readers wrote me asking, "What's next for our Hero?" Well, be sure to stay tuned because the saga of publishing Christian Fiction isn't quite over. Our Hero will be back in book two. Will he have more power? I sure hope so.

When I wrote *The Hero Within: Awareness,* I got many letters from fans thanking me for the book. Some had opinions adventures, while others simply rooted for Anthony.

As an author, I love feedback. Candidly, you're the reason I will explore the Hero's future. So tell me what you liked, what you loved, even what you hated. You can write me at comments@christianhero.org and visit me on the web at www.christianhero.org.

Finally, I need to ask a favor. If you're so inclined, I'd love a review of *The Hero Within: Awareness.* Loved it, hated it—I'd just enjoy your feedback.

Reviews can be tough to come by these days, and you, the reader, have the power to make or break a book. If you have the time, ***here's a link to my author page, along with all my books on Amazon:*** http://amzn.to/19p3dNx

Thank you so much for reading *The Hero Within: Awareness* and for spending time with me.

In gratitude,

Yeral E. Ogando

Turn the page to read the first chapter in *The Hero Within: Power*

For if a man think himself to be something, when he is nothing, he deceiveth himself. Galatians 6:3 (KJV)

## Chapter 1

Anthony Markson was ashamed to have led his team into such a trap. While some of the others were severely wounded, he had to admit, his worst injuries were to his pride.

"*Pride goeth before destruction,*" how well he knew. But how painful was the lesson.

The others could remember nothing but the horror and darkness they had gone through in the locked room.

As they sat in the emergency room, Anthony's eardrums felt ready to explode from the pain. The strange sound building in his ears almost drowned out other things he desperately needed to hear. Like the questions the doctor and nurse asked him.

He needed to clear his head and help the team before fear overtook and claimed them all.

~*~

The ER buzzed with activity. Nurse Erin Ludwig could barely keep up as she went from one cubical to another.

As if things weren't bad enough, that horney Tadd James had brought in her best friend Abby Power, along with three other injured people.

1

He said something about a dark room and vampire bats. *A likely story.* Erin would investigate the real reason that left Abby severely hurt with a broken arm and injures all over her once beautiful face.

Not long ago, Erin had advised Abby to set her boundaries when Tadd began to come on too strong with his interest.

"These teeth marks are huge," Erin said as she cleansed Abby's wounds with virus-killing liquid. "Could they really be from bats?"

If Tadd was to blame for Abby's wounds, he would definitely hear more from her.

Erin suspected Anthony would have some answers, and when she was finished here, she would question him further, along with the others who'd come in with them.

"This patient needs to be admitted," the doctor said. "Get an injection of HRIG ready."

"Did anyone think to bring one of the creatures in with the victims? Either way, we better get the procedure started to check for rabies."

"Find out exactly where this building is and notify the authorities to check it for bats. Depending on their findings we may have to treat the other patients in this group for rabies as a precaution."

~*~

In the next cubical, Dr. Sandra Beazel revealed a swollen ankle, and bruises all over her body.

# Power

"Can you tell us what happened?" Erin asked.

"Five of us went to Slattersville to check out office space to rent. We didn't expect it to be so dark in the building, but without the electricity hooked up—" She sighed. "Anyway, I fell into a hole in the floor and as you can see I hurt my ankle."

"I'll send you to x-ray first and see what we need to do for your ankle," the ER doctor said.

Erin touched Sandra's forearm. "And Abby? Did she fall into a hole as well?"

~*~

Erin and the doctor moved to the next cubical to check out a man named Chris Walker.

He was bruised and battered and could hardly move. They suspected a head injury when nothing he said made any sense.

The doctor recommended pain medicine for Chris while they checked the other patients.

~*~

Tadd James had more cuts than Erin had noticed when he'd arrived in the ER.

"Let me clean these wounds."

"How is Abby? Is she going to be all right?"

"You know I can't discuss the other patients with you." Erin tried to hold back her irritation with the man. After all, everyone who came to this hospital deserved the best care and courtesy.

~*~

After Sandra came back from x-ray Erin cleaned

her bruises.

"You are one lucky lady," the ER doctor said. "Your ankle is fractured but all the bones are in place."

"So I get a cast? Can I choose a pretty color like the children often get now days?"

"I see you have a sense of humor. But with the swelling you have we are going to use a brace first. We will check on you weekly. We may apply a cast when the swelling goes down."

"So how long—"

"No weight bearing on the ankle for a minimum of six weeks."

"Crutches?"

"Well if your insurance will go for it we have the hands free crutch with a pad to hold your leg bent at the knee and straps to your thigh. Or the knee scooter, but that one is a little more pricy, and won't leave your hands free."

~*~

By the time they checked on Chris again he was feeling better, but still seemed unable to understand what had happened.

The ER doctor took Erin aside and discussed the situation with her. "Since we don't know the man, perhaps he is simply one who is easily confused."

"You mean he may always be *a brick short of a load?*"

"Well, yes. To put it bluntly. On the other hand he

may be in shock. But the symptoms don't really add up to it being entirely that either."

"So, will you admit him?"

The doctor approached Chris's bed. "Our rooms are pretty full. If you have someone at home to watch over you tonight I can write you up a prescription and send you home."

"I share a small apartment with Anthony Markson. Will he be released as well?"

"I'll let you know."

~*~

"How are they?" Anthony asked as the ER doctor approached him. "How is our group holding up?"

"We have the rest of your team patched up for now. Just to be on the safe side we better examine you as well."

Anthony held out his arms. "As you can see I don't have a scratch on me."

"Will you be able to watch over your housemate, Chris Parker?"

"Of course."

"Okay, here is what you have to do." The ER doctor went over the symptoms for Anthony to watch for. "Wake him up every hour."

When the paperwork was finished and Tadd and Chris were released, Anthony assured Erin they would be back to check on Abby in the morning.

Yeral E. Ogando comes from a very humble origin and continues to be a humble servant of our Lord Almighty; understanding that we are nothing but vessels and the Lord who called us, also sends us to do His work, not our work. *Luke 17:10 "So likewise ye, when ye shall have done all those things which are commanded you, say, We are unprofitable servants: we have done that which was our duty to do."*

Mr. Ogando was born in the Caribbean, Dominican Republic. He is the beloved father of two beautiful girls Yeiris & Tiffany.

Jesus brought him to His feet at the age of 16-17. Since then, he has served as Co-pastor, pastor, Bible School teacher, youth counselor, and church planter. He is currently serving as the Secretary for the Dominican Reformed Church as well as the liaison for Haiti and USA.

Fluent in several languages Mr. Ogando is the Creator and owner of an Online Translation Ministry operating since 2007; with Native Christian translators in more than 25 countries.

(www.christian-translation.com),

The most exciting thing about his Translation Ministry is that thousands of people are receiving the Word of God in their native language on a daily basis and hundreds of ministries are able to reach the world through the work of Christian-Translation.com along with his translation network of 17 websites in different languages related to Christian Translation.

**Reviews:**
*Reviews can be tough to come by these days, and you, the reader, have the power to make or break a book. If you have the time, share your review or comments with me.*

Thank you so much for reading ***Awareness The Hero Within Volume One*** and for spending time with me. You can check out my other books and future books on my amazon page:

https://www.amazon.com/author/yeralogando

www.ingramcontent.com/pod-product-compliance
Lightning Source LLC
Chambersburg PA
CBHW020231180626
46810CB00006B/2134